ADVANCE PRAISE FOR

HOUSE CALL

"Ty Schwamberger is (not so) quietly establishing a reputation for producing lean, mean tales of true horror. He is a presence in the genre who warrants your attention and appreciation." —Tom Monteleone, 5-time winner of the Bram Stoker ® Award

"*House Call* is suspenseful and chilling, in that 'this thing could actually happen' kind of way. It reminded me of some of the best work of Laymon and Koontz, and moves like a rocket!" —Paul Kane, bestselling and award-winning author of *Before, Arcana*, and *Sherlock Holmes and the Servants of Hell*

"Dark, edgy, and quickly-paced, Ty Schwamberger's *House Call* is an unsettling, don't-answer-the-door chiller that's sharp as a razor, and just as deadly." —Greg F. Gifune, author of *Midnight Solitaire* and *God Machine*

"With *House Call*, Ty Schwamberger raises his game to a new level. Oozing suspense and dread, Schwamberger brings horror home with a violent tale of a sister and brother fighting for their lives against an all too human evil. Highly recommended." —Brett Talley, author of *He Who Walks In Shadow* and *The Fiddle is the Devil's Instrument*

"The ultimate 90s throwback—who put a slasher film in the *Home Alone* case at Blockbuster? It was Ty Schwamberger, splicing the best of the VHS era together!" —Nick Mamatas, author of *The Second Shooter* and *Sabbath*

HOUSE CALL

TY SCHWAMBERGER

JOURNALSTONE
YOUR LINK TO ARTIST TALENT

ISBN: 978-1-950305-77-3 (sc)
ISBN: 978-1-950305-78-0 (ebook)
Library of Congress Control Number: 2020952576

First printing edition: February 12, 2021
Published by JournalStone Publishing in the United States of America.
Cover Design and Layout: Don Noble
Edited by Sean Leonard
Proofreading and Interior Layout by Scarlett R. Algee

JournalStone Publishing
3205 Sassafras Trail
Carbondale, Illinois 62901

JournalStone books may be ordered through booksellers or by contacting:
JournalStone | www.journalstone.com

For the entire cast & crew of the film *House Call*.
You are all evilly awesome.

HOUSE
CALL

CHAPTER 1

WHEN VINCE'S FEVER reached 103 degrees, Mariam decided it was finally time to call a doctor. The fever had steadily risen throughout the night, despite aspirin and other over-the-counter fever-reducing medicines; now that it had gotten this high, Mariam knew that if she didn't do something soon, Vince would continue to worsen. Her parents were away for the weekend and had left her in charge to take care of Vince, even if that meant calling their family physician at this hour.

Leaving the door open a crack, Mariam left her brother's room and started for the staircase leading downstairs. As she walked down the dark hallway, she thought about what her parents would say if they found out that Vince was sick and they hadn't been informed. At the same time, Mariam knew that they were really looking forward to a weekend by themselves, and she didn't want to bother them unless absolutely necessary. *Hell, I can take care of this myself*, Mariam said to herself as she started down the staircase. *Besides, Mom and Dad trusted me enough to take care of things while they were away. All I have to do is call the doctor, he'll come over and give Vince some medicine, and he'll be good as new and Mom and Dad will never know the difference.* As she thought this, Mariam also remembered how her mom had called out the window of the car as they were pulling away to call them on her cellphone if they needed anything. Mariam was certain that she had only said that "in case of emergency" and not if someone had come down with the sniffles or a slight fever. *But this is definitely more than a runny nose or a slight fever*, Mariam thought. *Vince is really hurting up there, and Mom and Dad will probably be pissed if I don't at least call them and let them know what's going on.*

Mariam rounded the bottom of the stairs and headed toward the kitchen, where the phone was located.

Aside from the few streaks of moonlight coming in through the windows, the house was dark. If it wasn't her house, Mariam was certain she would be bumping into furniture on her way through the dining room and into the kitchen. But she had lived there ever since she was a little girl, so she knew the layout well even in near-complete darkness.

She entered the kitchen and started across the tile floor to the phone hanging on the wall by the back door.

She reached the phone, picked it up, and started punching in the number to the hotel in the city where her mom and dad were staying. On the third ring, someone picked up.

"Thank you for calling Paradise Hotel, my name is Gene, how may I help you?"

Mariam hung up.

Even with her parents more than likely wanting to know what was going on, it was late and they were probably asleep. *Either that or busy doing something I don't want to think about*, Mariam said to herself, picking the phone back up from its base on the wall.

She punched in a new set of numbers and waited. The other end of the line rang five or six times. Mariam was about ready to forget about it and hang up the phone when a groggy-sounding woman's voice came across the receiver.

"Hel…hello…"

"Ah, yes, Mrs. Blythworth, this is Mariam Oster, my family are patients of your husband's."

Mariam heard the sleepy woman give a deep huff and then the line went quiet for a few seconds. The next voice that came across the phone was a deep male voice.

"Hello. This is Dr. Blythworth. Who did you say you were again?"

"Oh, hi, Dr. Blythworth. This is Mariam Oster. I'm Robert and Julia's daughter."

"Oh, yes. What seems to be the trouble, Mariam?"

"You know my brother Vince? He's a patient of yours as well and, ummm… He's not feeling very well, and…"

The doctor cut in. "Mariam, it is late. Why don't you have your parents call my office in the morning and schedule an appointment, and I'll see your brother at that time. If this is an emergency, I suggest you tell your parents to take Vince to the ER. I can follow up with the hospital in the morning for your brother's status."

"That's sorta the problem, Dr. Blythworth," Mariam said.

"What is?"

"My parents. See, they're out of town for the weekend and left me in charge. They really don't want to be bothered. Plus I told them if anything did come up, I would handle it myself."

"I see."

"And, well…Vince just came down with something tonight. It was after dinner and he started complaining about his stomach not feeling very well. I told him to take some pink stuff and go lay down. He seemed to be doing fine until a few hours ago. But that's when the fever came. It's gone up each hour ever since.

"So, you see, Dr. Blythworth…I really can't call my parents. They'll never let me stay home alone with Vince again if I don't take care of this myself."

"I see. Well, in that case, why don't you just take your brother to the ER by yourself? If I remember correctly, you're sixteen now."

"Yes, Doctor…I *am* sixteen, but I only have my temps right now. Mom and Dad are taking me next weekend to take my driving test. Plus, even if I did have my license, Mom and Dad took the only car, so I couldn't take Vince to the ER even if I wanted to."

Dr. Blythworth didn't reply right away. Instead, Mariam could hear him and his wife talking in the background. A moment later there was a ruffling sound like he was taking his hand away from the phone, and his voice returned.

"Okay, Mariam. I tell you what. I don't make house calls, haven't for years, but because of your situation I'll make an exception this time. What's your address?"

Mariam gave the doctor her address and was about to say thank you, but he replied with a quick, "Okay, got it. See you in thirty minutes," and hung up.

What a jerk, Mariam said to herself as she hung up the phone and walked over to the fridge to get something to drink. *We've been going to him as long as I can remember, you'd think he would be a little nicer than that.*

But Mariam knew she was being too hard on the doctor. She knew that if it were the other way around, she too would have suggested other alternatives before deciding to make a house call in the middle of the night. Especially with it starting to rain.

As Mariam drew a pitcher of lemonade out of the fridge, she could hear the first pitter-pats of rain on the outside of the house's windows. She took a tall glass from the cupboard, filled it three-fourths of the way with the sweet yellow liquid, and then put the pitcher back into the fridge. She then set the glass on the counter, opened up the freezer, and took out a box of Popsicles. She pulled out a red one, Vince's favorite, and then put the box back in the freezer. Grabbing her glass of lemonade and carrying the Popsicle, she headed back through the kitchen and dining room and started up the stairs toward Vince's room.

She wanted to tell her little brother to hold on for just a while longer, that a doctor was on the way.

CHAPTER 2

TAKING A SIP from her lemonade, Mariam pushed Vince's door open and walked into the room. It reeked of sweat and body odor. A small nightlight was on, casting an eerie glow over the small lump in the bed. Mariam walked up to the bed, put her glass on the nightstand, and leaned over her nine-year-old brother.

"Vince...you awake...I thought you might like a Popsicle," Mariam said, gently shaking her brother.

"Huh? Wha..."

"It's me, Mariam. Sorry to wake you, but I thought it would be a good idea to check your temperature again."

"Oh, okay," Vince replied, pushing himself up and leaning against the headboard.

Mariam took the thermometer off the nightstand, wiped its metal tip off with a Kleenex, and put it under Vince's tongue.

A minute later the thermometer gave off a beep, telling Mariam that it was done calculating her brother's temperature. She pulled it from Vince's mouth and looked it at.

103.5 degrees.

Damn.

"Well, what is it?" Vince asked, pulling a comforter up to his sweaty neck. "'Cause I think I'm feeling a little better now."

Mariam pushed a button on the thermometer to turn it off.

"Well, it looks like it's going up. So you better have this," Mariam said, handing the Popsicle to her brother.

"Wow, thanks. Red, my favorite."

Mariam picked up her lemonade from the nightstand and took another drink. The sugary lemon water was bitter, but tasted wonderful.

"I've got some good news," Mariam said, setting her glass back down onto the nightstand.

"Mom and Dad are coming home?"

"No. Not that. I called Dr. Blythworth and he said he's coming over to take a look at you."

"Oh. Don't you think it's a better idea to have Mom and Dad come home?"

"Nah. This'll be fine. Besides, I told Mom and Dad that I could handle taking care of you and the house while they have a relaxing weekend alone together."

"Still. I think you should call Mom and Dad and at least let them know what's going on," Vince said, taking another lick from the melting Popsicle.

"Nah, this'll be fine. The doctor will come over, take a look at you, and probably give you some sort of medicine to feel better. Then we don't have to call Mom and Dad and wake them up. By the time they get home on Sunday, you'll be feeling better and no one will be the wiser."

"Yeah, I guess that will work. But what if Dr. Blythworth mentions something to Mom or Dad at one of their next appointments? Then how are you going to explain to them that I had a 103-degree temperature and you didn't call them?"

Mariam didn't know the answer to that, so instead of replying to her brother's question, she shrugged her shoulders, picked up her lemonade, and started toward the bedroom door.

"Hey, where are you going?" Vince asked.

"I gotta pee. Besides, I won't be able to hear Dr. Blythworth at the door when he gets here if I am sitting up here in your room."

"Don't worry though," Mariam continued, "he said he wouldn't be long. But, if he is taking a while to get here, I'll come back up and check on you again. Okay?"

As she left the room and made her way back downstairs to use the bathroom, Mariam heard her brother mumble, "Okay," while sucking on his Popsicle.

After urinating and flushing the toilet, Mariam washed her hands, threw some cold water on her face to fight off how tired she felt, picked up her lemonade from the counter, and made her way down the hall, past the stairs on her left, and turned right into the living room. It was dark except for a low-wattage lamp sitting on a small table at the far end of the room, the one her mother always left on whether they were home or not. Mariam figured it was her mother's way of showing that someone was home, whether or not anyone truly was.

She walked by her father's rocker, set her glass on the coffee table, and plopped down on the couch. Her eyes were heavy and felt like they were going to close by themselves, whether Mariam wanted them to or not. She gently slapped her face a few times and then picked up the remote and turned on the television. She started to flip through the channels, hoping to catch a late-night Jerry Springer or Steve Harvey marathon, but didn't see that either was on. She settled for an infomercial about a sandwich maker.

After a few minutes of watching a middle-aged man and woman talk about how easy the portable oven was to use and clean, her eyes started to get heavy again. She tried a few times keeping herself awake by forcing her eyes open really wide, but as soon as her lids touched the bottom of her eye, she felt herself drifting to sleep.

After a few more minutes of trying to fight it off, her eyes closed all the way, and she drifted off.

CHAPTER 3

SHE HEARD THE scream and then she was running. Up the stairs, down the hallway, and into her brother's room.

Even with only the small glow from the nightlight, Mariam could tell that her brother wasn't in bed. The lump that had formed Vince's body was gone. The comforter looked like it had been pushed into a pile at the foot of the bed. She scanned the room. Nothing. She noticed a small, dark, round object in the middle of the bed, but figured it was nothing more than one of Vince's stuffed animals. She heard the pattering of rain outside against the windows.

"Vince? Where are you?"

There was no answer.

Maybe he fell asleep, had a bad dream, and is now hiding in the closet. Mariam knew her brother had done it before, and it was possible it had happened again.

Mariam walked back over to the bedroom door. She could hear the rain coming down harder now. It almost sounded like the roof had come off the house and it was raining inside. She reached up and flicked the light switch. The overhead light came on and filled the room. Mariam blinked a few times, hoping her eyes would soon adjust.

When her vision finally cleared, she stood facing Vince's bed. As she had noticed while the room was near-dark, her brother wasn't lying in it. In his place was a dark puddle in the middle of the bed. At first Mariam thought that Vince had just wet the bed and was probably in the bathroom getting cleaned up. But that thought didn't last for long. Oh, no. As Mariam stared at the bed, she finally noticed where the loud pattering of rain was coming from.

It was from above the bed.

Where Vince was hanging by his neck. His belly had been sliced open. His innards were on the outside. Blood was running down his legs, to his toes, then dripping into the bloody puddle in the middle of the bed.

Mariam screamed and collapsed onto the floor.

* * *

When Mariam awoke, she was drenched in sweat. *Thank God, it was only a nightmare*, she told herself, lifting her head from a pillow on the couch. She stood up, stretched her arms over her head, and looked at the clock on the mantel above the fireplace. It read 12:17. It had been an hour since she talked to Dr. Blythworth on the phone. He said he would be there in thirty minutes. Maybe he's running late or having trouble finding the house, Mariam thought, walking out of the living room and starting up the stairs.

Even though it was only a nightmare, I better check on Vince.

Mariam rounded the top of the stairs and walked into Vince's bedroom. The bed was empty. Her heart started to pound in her ears. *This can't be happening.* She reached over and flicked on the light. To her relief, her brother wasn't hanging, gutted, over the bed. Nor was there a dark, bloody spot on the sheets.

She let out a sigh of relief.

But where could her brother be? That was what started to bother Mariam. *If he came downstairs to use the bathroom, he probably would have woken me up. Then again, maybe he realized how worn out I was after taking care of him all night, so instead of bothering me, he might have decided to just let me rest. But he knew I was going to be waiting downstairs for Dr. Blythworth. I would think he would have come over and shaken me, told me to stay awake and wait for him.*

In any event, her brother was missing from his room and she needed to find him.

I'm sure he's probably just in the bathroom using the toilet or brushing his teeth or something.

She turned out of the room and started back down the stairs.

She turned right and walked down the hallway, which went from the front of the house to the back, where the only bathroom in the house was located, along with the laundry room. As she neared the end of the hallway, the laundry room was dark, but there was a crack of light coming from under the bathroom door.

She went up to the bathroom door and knocked.

"Vince...you in there? You okay?"

She heard a rustling sound on the other side of the door but no response from her brother.

She knocked again. No response.

"Hey, Vince. It's me, Mariam. I'm going to come in. Okay?"

Just as she was twisting the knob on the bathroom door, she heard another rustling sound. Then Vince said, "No, wait. Don't come in! I'm using the toilet right now."

"Oh. Oh, okay. Well, take your time and let me know if you need anything, sweetie. I'll be in the kitchen."

Mariam heard her brother say, "Okay, thanks," as she let go of the doorknob and started back down the hallway.

CHAPTER 4

MARIAM HAD DECIDED to give it ten more minutes before giving the doctor another call to see what was taking him so long. She didn't want to be a bother, but also needed to know that he was indeed on the way and didn't accidently fall back asleep after they got off the phone with one another. She stood up from the breakfast bar she had been sitting at while drinking a cup of hot cocoa, walked over to the wall phone, and picked up the receiver.

She punched in the doctor's number and waited.

Five...six...seven rings went off in her ear. No one picked up the other end of the line.

Damn.

Either he did fall back asleep and turned off the ringer so he wouldn't be bothered, or he's on his way over and his wife doesn't feel like picking up the phone again in the middle of the night. Whatever the reason, Mariam had a knot in the pit of her stomach. If the doctor did fall asleep, she thought, and doesn't come over, Mom and Dad will definitely find out that Vince's sick, think I didn't do anything to help him, and get pissed at me.

Won't be getting my license if that happens, Mariam said to herself, putting the phone back in its cradle and walking out of the kitchen.

She walked through the dark dining room and stopped in the front entrance-way. Small beams of light were coming from the vertical windows on each side of the front door. The windows themselves were double-paned with a crisscross design etched into them.

She walked up to the window on the left and looked out.

The street directly in front of her house was dark and wet from the rain. Only a floating mist from the downpour was still visible in the streetlights. Her driveway was empty. There were a few cars parked on the street, despite the city ordinance not to do so. Mariam figured they were cars of one of her neighbors' friends that were in town for the weekend; they probably didn't know nor care about this particular residential street's parking laws. She also noticed there were lights on across the street at the Henderson house. Probably Mr. Henderson watching some sort of dirty movie on the boob-tube, Mariam thought.

He's one sick puppy!

It was just a guess that it was Mr. Henderson and not his eighteen-year-old son that was up at such an hour. But she was pretty sure that it was Mister, since she didn't see Junior's car in the driveway. She also wasn't entirely sure that the man in the house across the street was watching a porno or Skin-A-Max, but she was pretty sure of that, too. She didn't really know much about him, except that the way he sometimes looked at her, especially when her parents weren't around, gave her the willies.

It was late last summer, and she was fifteen at the time. One of her chores was to wash the family car. Mariam didn't mind it though. She enjoyed being outside rather than in the stuffy house when it was nice and hot out. And since it was so nice out, she had decided to put on her yellow and blue polka-dotted bikini so she could also work on her tan while washing the Mercedes. It was a win-win situation, really.

She put on the bikini, trotted downstairs, grabbed a SunnyD out of the fridge, and headed out to the garage to gather the necessary car-care items—a bucket, sponge, car soap, a chamois, and a few dirty rags for drying her hands. She then walked out the open garage door to the side of the house, turned on the water, and dragged the hose to the front.

While she rinsed and soaped the car, she hoped that one of the older boys in her school would drive by and see how she looked in her bikini. She had always been shy around the boys in school, but over this particular summer she had really blossomed and had come into her own as far as her body was concerned. So, as she scrubbed the dead bugs and tar from the car, she constantly peered over her shoulder, hoping someone would drive by. Of course, they never did. But even without a car driving by, she felt like someone had been watching her. Sure enough, one of the times she was bent over in front of the car with her back to the street, she turned her head and saw Mr. Henderson coming across the street toward her. He was carrying a can of soda in one hand, a beer in the other, and had a goofy grin stretched across his face. Mariam had quickly stood up when she saw him crossing the street and put her hands in front of her crotch to conceal herself, but knew that she was showing a lot of skin and couldn't really do much about it anyway. Hell, she had thought, it's not like he didn't already get an eye-full if he's been watching me the whole time. She took her hands away from her front and threw the dirty sponge in the bucket. Mr. Henderson finished crossing the street and stopped a few feet in front of her.

"Hey there, Mariam. How's it going?"

"Ah, not too bad, Mr. Henderson. Nice day, eh?"

"Yeah, but sure is a hot one. Thought you could use a drink," he said, holding out the can of soda for Mariam to take.

"Oh, no thanks, Mr. Henderson. I've got a SunnyD over there by the garage door. But thanks anyway."

"Oh, come on. Take it. It's nice and cold. Heck, you've been out here for a while now…"

So he has been watching me this whole time, Mariam said to herself.

"…so that drink of yours is probably warm by now."

Mariam just shrugged.

"So, anyway…how's your summer going?"

Ugh. Doesn't this guy ever stop? "Anyway, Mr. Henderson…thanks for the offer, but I've really got to finish scrubbing and rinse this sucker before the suds dry and leave water marks on the car."

She thought he was going to leave after that, but he didn't. Instead, he just backed up a few feet to the sidewalk and stopped. Mariam had wanted to run inside and hide in her room, or at least tell her mom that the creepy pervert from across the street was outside gawking at her, but figured she better get to finishing the car before the suds did dry and leave marks. She knew her father wouldn't like it if that happened, especially since the car was brand new and he had only just bought it a few weeks ago. So instead of running inside for her mommy, Mariam decided to "be a big girl" and finish the car, even with Mr. Henderson blatantly staring at her when she had to bend over to reach the middle of the car with the sponge. At one point she even noticed him drooling a little and something poking against the underside of his khaki shorts. He was getting turned on watching her, but she had a job to do and decided to just push through the embarrassment and get it done as quick as possible. Then she could go inside and never, ever come outside in her bikini again.

Damn, if he could only see me now, Mariam said to herself as she stood at the window and continued to watch for Dr. Blythworth's car to pull into their driveway. *Ugh. What the hell am I thinking? "If he could only see me now"? What the hell is that all about? I don't want that sicko staring at my goods!* But at the same time, she knew that she looked good. Hell, she knew she looked great, having "grown" even more over the past year. If he could only see me now, she thought. I'd probably give him a heart attack!

Sick bastard would deserve it, too!

She shook her head and chuckled at the thought. Then she backed away from the window and headed upstairs to check on her sick brother.

CHAPTER 5

WHEN MARIAM ARRIVED in her brother's room, it still reeked of sweat and body odor, but there was a new smell present as well. At first Mariam didn't recognize it, but she soon realized that her brother must have grabbed the vapor rub from the bathroom and applied it to his body. Using the vapor rub the times Mariam had been sick in the past had always seemed to do the trick, especially if she had a bad cough or her nose was stuffy. She really hoped that Vince wasn't coming down with something even worse, besides the belly ache and fever. She also wished that Dr. Blythworth would get a move on and arrive soon. Though, she was starting to doubt that he was even coming at all.

Maybe he did fall back asleep. I guess I could give him another call and find out if he's left yet.

She didn't like the idea of calling the doctor's house at such an hour, but she had to do something to get Vince feeling better, and soon.

She walked over, kissed her brother on the forehead, then walked out of the room and stood in the hallway. Even though she wasn't doing much physical activity, taking care of her brother and watching out for Dr. Blythworth was beginning to make her tired again.

Maybe I'll just go to my room and rest my eyes for a few minutes.

It sounded like a wonderful idea, but she knew that if she did go into her room and shut her eyes, it could turn out to be hours—maybe she would even sleep until the next morning—and she would not hear Dr. Blythworth at the door. If he would indeed make the house call that he had promised. No. She knew that she had to go downstairs and try to call the doctor again, even if it meant making his wife or him upset. She had to get some help, and fast, for Vince.

The hell with it, she said to herself, *I've gotta find out what is taking him so long.*

She walked down the hallway and stairs, through the dining room, and entered the still-dark kitchen. She thought about turning on the overhead light, but didn't really see a reason to. The small light coming from the exhaust hood over the stovetop was enough that she could see what she was doing anyway. She left the doorway and made her way over to the phone. She picked it up and started to dial the doctor's home number.

Right when a connection was made, and she thought she heard the doctor's wife on the other end, the doorbell rang. She slammed the phone down on its cradle and rushed to the front door. She grabbed the doorknob and was about to unlock the deadbolt with her other hand when she decided to first check *who* was at the door.

One can never be too careful.

She put her eye up to the peephole.

And saw another eye staring back at her.

She screamed.

Arms flying and legs staggering backwards, Mariam was still screaming when her butt hit the floor. She took a deep breath and let it out. Assuming it was just Dr. Blythworth at the front door, she picked herself up, unlocked the inner door, and swung it toward herself.

It was indeed Dr. Blythworth. Mariam could tell that much. He had thinning brown hair with silver specks, a brown wool jacket and grey slacks. He was clutching a black bag in his right hand. But what Mariam didn't understand was why he was leaning against the screen door. He was against it in such a way that if he put any more of his weight onto it, he would rip the screen and crash right through. *Maybe he's just tired*, Mariam said to herself, stepping up to the door and taking a good look at the top of Dr. Blythworth's head.

"Dr. Blythworth…you okay?" Mariam said, tapping a finger on the doctor's head through the screen.

Damn. He's out like a light.

"Doctor…" was all Mariam could get out as the physician's body fell away from the screen and slumped to the porch floor. His head connected with the porch with a thump. "Oh my God…Doctor…"

Mariam tried to push open the screen door to attend to the doctor, which was a strange twist of events in her mind, but his feet were in the way. She could only push the door open a few inches. "Doctor, please..." Mariam said, putting her weight against the door and pushing. The doctor's legs began to bend, letting the screen door open enough for Mariam to squeeze out of the house. She peered down at the man. He wasn't moving. Without getting closer, and without a light, Mariam couldn't even tell if he was breathing or not. She pulled open the screen door, reached around the door jamb, and flicked the porch light on.

She screamed again as she watched the blood flow out of a deep gash in the doctor's neck.

The blood began to run off the porch and down the front steps.

CHAPTER 6

"I STILL DON'T know about this."

John heard his friend in the passenger's seat say something, but wasn't really listening to him. He was too busy laughing at the sight of the teenage girl on the front porch of the house across the street trying to deal with the dead guy. It was the same guy that he had killed a few minutes ago by slashing his throat with a razor. Killing someone had always been sort of a hobby for John, but actually getting to see someone's reaction to his handiwork was putting an extra smile on his face now. He turned to his friend.

"Huh? What did you say?"

"I said I don't know about this. I mean…it's one thing to break into people's homes and steal their shit, but this is going a little far, don't you think?"

"You worry too much, man," John replied, taking the last hit on his cigarette and flicking the butt into the street. "Besides, I told you there is some prime shit in that house. It'll bring us some major coinage with Smitty at the pawn shop…so why you bitchin'?"

"'Cause, man," stuttered Nick, "I didn't sign up to be a part of no murder. Shit. You killed that dude in cold blood."

"Hey, you want part of the take or not, man?"

"Never said I didn't."

"Shit. You might as well. You're over there complaining about *me* cutting some asshole's throat… Hell, you didn't even know the guy."

"Doesn't matter if I knew him or not…you still didn't have to kill him."

"Sure as shit did. We cased out this house for a reason, remember? 'Cause we knew that the kid's parents were gonna be gone for at least tonight, hell, maybe the whole weekend… We can not only rob the place, but have a little fun at the same time. Besides, do you really think if we broke in there, that he wouldn't have put up a fight?"

"Well…yeah…I mean…I'm sure he would have…but still…we could have tied him up or something."

"Yeah, well…whatever, man."

John didn't want to argue anymore. The only thing he cared about was waiting for the girl to quit messing with the dead guy and to go call the cops. He wanted to laugh out loud at the idea of the girl running into the house and picking up the phone, only to find out it didn't have a dial tone—the phone lines had been cut—and she wouldn't be able to call for help. He let out a snort, instead. He then pulled another cigarette from his pack and lit it with the car lighter. He took a deep pull on the cancer stick and blew the smoke out his nose.

As he watched the girl across the street try to figure out what to do next, John thought back to the first time he had been involved in killing someone to get what he wanted.

It had only been six months ago, but it felt more like six years. He had done dozens more jobs since then. Some by himself. Others with his buddy Nick, who was now sitting in the seat next to him.

Breaking into people's homes was never a problem for John. He never thought twice about it. He had gone from breaking into his classmates' lockers at school, to his parent's safe, then to cars, and finally graduated on to houses. It was a thrill for him. Always had been. But he still had no idea what a thrill it *truly* was until he broke into that young couple's house six months ago.

He had been sitting in a car across the street from a house, similar to the one he was staring at now, with his mentor, so to speak. His name was Rock. John never knew his real name. But he knew that people called him Rock because he had a reputation for being a real hard ass. That night, when they broke into the house together, he got first-hand experience why his name truly fit him.

Rock and John had, of course, done the preliminary surveillance on the house that was necessary for any successful break-in. They took note when the husband, or who they thought was the husband, left for work in the morning, leaving his wife alone in the house. They found out later that it was not the husband leaving for work, but actually the son leaving for school.

As they quietly worked the back door open with a crowbar and entered the house, they instantly knew something wasn't right. They heard screaming coming from the upstairs of the house. Figuring that someone had maybe beaten them to the take, they crept upstairs to find the husband and wife locked in some sort of twisted position. The man was making the woman scream with delight as he worked his hard cock in and out of her. Rock entered the bedroom first, a hard kick sending the cracked door flying open. Then he charged in. John tried to stay right behind him, but he was just too quick. In what seemed like one motion, Rock ran to the bed, sliced the man's throat with a straight razor, and threw him off his wife, who was now choking from all the blood raining down upon her from the deep gash in her husband's neck. John had thought that the woman was a good screamer before seeing her husband killed before her very eyes. But that was just the beginning. Once she noticed she was no longer getting pounded by her husband's cock, she opened her eyes wide, and then *really* started streaming. She started thrashing on the bed as well. But ol' Rock took care of her just as quickly as he had her husband. He reached down, pulled the woman closer to him by her hair, and then, holding the woman with his right hand, he folded and stuck the straight razor in his pocket with his left, pulled out his cock, and jammed it into her mouth. She grunted and choked a few times, especially when he came. After he was done, with his wet cock still hanging out the zipper of his pants, he whipped the razor back out, reached down, and sliced her from ear to ear. She stopped screaming after that.

After the incident in the bedroom, John and Rock did what they had come there to do. They robbed the place. They took jewels, silver, some colorful egg-looking things from the mantel above the fireplace that Rock said were valuable, and even took some CDs from the son's room. John didn't really understand why they were bothering with CDs. Rock explained that it was just for kicks; as he so delicately put it, "We'll show the little bastard what assholes we really are."

Even though seeing the couple murdered was more than John had ever wished to see, something inside him was aroused by the events that had taken place. He felt more alive, somehow, than he had ever felt before. From that point on, he knew he would look up to Rock, even if his life would only last a few more minutes.

Little did they know as they exited the house and started down the driveway to the getaway car parked across the street, but a nosey neighbor had heard the commotion next door and called the cops. They were quick on the scene, too. A little too quick for any response that John had ever seen before. But, regardless, as they started down the driveway, two marked patrol cars screeched to a halt in front of the house and the cops came jumping out with their guns drawn. They told Rock and him to stop. John froze; Rock didn't. As he continued walking down the driveway, he called over his shoulder to John, "Get outta here, man. Save yourself. They'll never take me alive. I'm never going back." With that, John turned and ran. He still wasn't sure to this very day if the cops saw him or if Rock was just too big of a distraction, with his 6'3", 280-pound body coming toward them. Then again, it probably didn't hurt his escape, as Rock was carrying his bag of loot in one hand and his open straight razor in the other, telling the cops, "Come on, pigs! Show me what you got."

As John ran from the scene, he only took the time to look over his shoulder once. It was enough to see Rock go down in a hail of gunfire. It must have taken a shitload of bullets to bring him down; John heard a multitude of shots go off as he ran through the back yard of the couple's house, into the alley, and then hightailed it out of the area.

Even though it had been a hell of a way for Rock to die, John still knew that he had been taught well by his mentor.

As he ran down the alley, he never lost hold of the bag that carried his part of the take from the house they had just robbed.

* * *

Now that he sat in his own car, next to *his* protégé, he knew that no matter what happened in the house tonight, he would be the sort of role model that Rock had been to him and show Nick how it was supposed to be done. He smiled.

Still staring at the house, he noticed the girl turn and run back inside.

To call the cops.

He continued to smile because he knew, this time, the cops wouldn't be coming to take *anyone* down.

This robbery was going to be a success.

He was sure of it.

CHAPTER 7

MARIAM DIDN'T KNOW what to do first. Should she check on Vince upstairs in his room, or run to the phone and call the police? Knowing in the back of her mind that it was her responsibility to take care of Vince, that is where she headed first.

Racing up the stairs, the image of the dead Dr. Blythworth with his throat cut raced through Mariam's mind. She tried to shake it off as she chugged up the stairs, but it was hard to do so. She had only seen one other dead body before: her grandfather, lying in a casket in a funeral home a few years back. He had been dressed perfectly in his favorite navy blue suit and was lying peacefully inside his eternal home. It was nothing like she had just seen on her front porch steps—Dr. Blythworth, the family doctor, who instead of helping her little brother, now lay in a puddle of his own blood. She pushed herself faster to the top of the stairs, rounded the corner, and raced into Vince's room.

As she had hoped, Vince was still in bed, asleep, oblivious to the horrible act that had been committed not far from the safe confines of his bedroom. Mariam raced over to her brother and shook his shoulder.

"Vince…wake up…something happened to Dr. Blythworth." She couldn't get out of her throat *what* exactly had occurred.

Her brother began to stir, opened his eyes and looked up. "Wha…what's going on?"

"The doctor…Dr. Blythworth…he's hurt bad…maybe even dead. We've got to get out of here!"

"What in the world are you talking about, Mariam?"

"Remember how I told you that Dr. Blythworth was coming over to take a look at you?"

"Yeah…so?"

"Well, he's here, all right…but…but somebody must have attacked him before I could get to the door…he's dead, Vince."

"*Dead?*"

"Yes. Now get your butt in gear, put on some clothes, and come with me."

A few moments later, Vince was scrambling out of bed and trying to find the clothes he had been wearing before he'd changed into his pajamas and climbed into bed for the night.

"Where's my Grave Digger shirt?" Vince said, as Mariam was peeking outside the door of his room, making sure no one was coming up the stairs.

"I don't *know*, Vince," Mariam screamed. "It doesn't really matter what you put on, just find something to cover yourself with."

As Vince looked for something else besides his favorite shirt, Mariam started to think of what they would do next. Her first thought was to hide somewhere in the house, maybe the basement, but she didn't like the idea of being trapped down there without an escape route. She had watched enough cop movies to know that the last thing you wanted to do when someone was in your house was to corner yourself in. She remembered seeing a movie once that starred Jodie Foster called *Panic Room*. In the movie, Jodie and her daughter were the victims of a break-in and had a special room to hide in so that whoever was in the house couldn't find them. And even if the bad guys did find them, there would be no way for them to get into the room because of how secure it was. Mariam wished they had one of those rooms now. But they didn't, and she would have to think of some other way to hide and protect Vince and herself from whoever had done that horrible thing to the good doctor.

A moment later, Vince was done getting dressed. Mariam waved to her brother to follow, and they raced down the hall to Mariam's bedroom. Since it was late at night, Mariam was wearing only a tank top and cotton shorts. They were probably the same clothes she would have gone to bed in, if she had ever gotten the opportunity to do so tonight. But now she knew she wouldn't get that chance. Not with the dead doctor on the front porch steps and God only knows who coming in after them. She ran over to her dresser and pulled open the second to last drawer.

Inside were clothes she might wear to school or out of the house on the weekends. Rifling through the items, she decided on a yellow chamois shirt and khaki shorts. She quickly put them on over her tank top and short cotton shorts. She put on a pair of running socks from her top drawer, then ran over to the closet to get her running shoes. She found them on top of the pile containing all her other shoes. As she sat down on the floor to put them on, she glanced up at her brother and saw the look of fear on his face. She felt sorry that Vince had to experience something such as this, but as long as they could find somewhere to hide until after the bad guys were gone, whoever they were, then everything would turn out okay. She quickly laced up her shoes, stood up, and went to the bedroom door.

Slowly peeking around the door jamb, Mariam scanned the dark hallway for movement. She didn't see any. She grabbed her brother by the hand and pulled him after her. That's when she heard the breaking of glass downstairs and, in that instant, knew this was for real and they would have to find someplace to hide.

But before finding a place to hide, she knew she had to call the police.

The problem was that the only phone in the house was in the kitchen, downstairs, the same place where people were breaking into the house.

CHAPTER 8

AFTER NICK HAD broken out one of the windows to the back door and reached through the pane to unlock it, they stepped into the house. They were in the kitchen. The room was dark except for a small light that was on above the stove. John walked over, broken glass crunching under his shoes, and turned it off. Only the faint light from the moon coming in through a small window above the sink helped them to see where they were going.

"Come on, man. Start looking around," John whispered to Nick.

"In the kitchen?"

"Hell yeah! You never know what sort of treasures people hide in strange places."

Nick just nodded back as he started to search the cabinet drawer that was closest to him. John went over to the fridge and pulled it open. A blast of light engulfed the room. He thought he heard Nick say, "Hey, man," but didn't pay attention. The intensity of jobs like this always made John's throat dry, so he was looking for something to quench his thirst. He pulled a few bottles from the fridge, closed the door, and turned back to his friend who was rummaging through the silverware drawer. John walked over and pressed the cold bottle of beer against the back of Nick's neck. He jumped.

"Hey, man...what the hell!"

"Oh, stop. It's just a beer, man. Enjoy."

Nick took the cold bottle of brew from John, twisted off the top, and took a few gulps. The beer was bitter and cold. It tasted wonderful. "This stuff is great. Thanks." John nodded and turned away to begin looking through some drawers. It wasn't always the case that you would find something valuable in the kitchen, but it was better to look and not find anything than to second guess yourself once you were back in the car and speeding away. He didn't find much in the first drawer, so he moved on to another one. He didn't find anything in that one either.

"Any luck over there?" John said over his shoulder as he took another drink of beer.

"Nah. Nothing here. How about you?"

"Nada."

After a few more minutes of searching the drawers and cabinets, John decided it was time to move on to the next room.

They walked out of the kitchen and into the dining room.

* * *

The first thing that John noticed when they walked into the room was a hutch in the far corner. He knew from experience that it was a good possibility there could be some plates and other knick-knacks that might be worth something in there. They walked over, pulled open the twin doors, and looked inside.

Though the dining room had a bay window that was letting in a fair amount of light, it was still difficult to see inside the hutch. John reached into his pocket and pulled out a pen light. Pushing a button on its top, a small line of light shot out the other end. It was small enough that if a neighbor were looking at the house from across the street it wouldn't be noticeable enough to cause concern, but it was bright enough to see things that were a foot or so in front of you with no problem at all.

"Oh, yeah…this is the good shit right here," John said, motioning to Nick to open the canvas bag they had brought in with them.

"Yeah, nice."

John proceeded to load the bag with collector's plates, trinkets that looked old and were probably worth something to somebody, and various other small items that he found in the hutch. By the time they were finished, only a few dust bunnies remained hiding in the hutch's back corners. John smiled. Even though the hutch was a nice score, he was sure that the house contained a lot more valuable things in the master bedroom upstairs. John waved his right hand and they proceeded out of the dining room.

They came to the entrance-way leading into the rest of the house.

As they stood there with the moon, street, and porch lights flooding in through the windows, they saw the dead guy still lying on the porch. John knew that if they let him lay there any longer, it was a strong possibility that a neighbor or someone driving by would notice. Hell, it was hard *not* to notice a 250-pound dead guy bleeding all over the place on a well-lit front porch.

"Hey, Nick."

"Yeah?"

"We need to get this fucker off the porch."

"Yeah, I was just thinking the same thing. But first things first. We need to kill that porch light."

"Good thinking," John answered, moving to the front door and thumbing down the light switch.

The porch went mostly dark.

Nick then put down his bag of goodies and followed John onto the front porch.

"You get his head and I'll get his feet."

"Right."

Nick reached under the guy's bloody head and grasped underneath his arms. John was bent over and grabbing the guy's ankles. "Okay, on the count of three. One…two…" The guy was heavy, so they were only able to lift him an inch or so off the porch, but it was enough for them to shuffle him into the house. John threw down the guy's legs and closed the door, then dead-bolted it.

"Damn, that guy was a heavy son of a bitch."

"Hell yeah. Makes me want to have another beer," John huffed.

"Sounds good to me. But, hey…what about the kids?"

"The hell with them. It's not like they're going anywhere, ya know. We might as well enjoy ourselves…we've got all night…who knows, maybe the whole weekend to enjoy the place…not that I expect to be here more than a few hours, but still."

"Yeah," Nick replied, "I guess you're right…the hell with them…let's get that beer…my treat."

The two men chuckled as they stepped over the body and headed back toward the kitchen.

CHAPTER 9

STANDING AT THE top of the stairs, Mariam and Vince could hear that someone was indeed in the house. They could hear them rummaging through items in the kitchen and dining room. It wasn't until they had dragged the body of Dr. Blythworth in from the front porch that they saw the two men who were inside their house. At first Mariam and Vince thought they would see them at the top of the stairs, but soon realized it was too dark in the house for that. Then they were worried that the two men might turn around and start to climb the stairs, which would put them face to face with each other. The whole ordeal scared both of them. They didn't know what to do next. Since the men had walked away from the front door and back into the kitchen to drink more of their dad's beer, should they try to creep down the stairs and escape out the front door, or should they just stay put until another alternative presented itself? They had no idea.

"So, what do you think?" Vince asked in a quiet voice.

"I don't know, sweetie. I really don't. I mean...at first, I thought we should go downstairs and try to get out the front door. But they locked it. If we try to go down there and unlock the door, they might hear the sound of the bolt snapping back, no matter how quiet we try to be, ya know? Plus, the time it takes us to creep down the stairs, they might finish in the kitchen and catch us in mid-step...and we definitely don't want that."

"Yeah."

"Besides...I'm pretty sure those are the two men that killed Dr. Blythworth, and I wouldn't put it past them to do the same to us if they find out we're in the house."

"What if they already know we're in here?"

"Well, I really don't think they know we are, ya know? 'Cause if they did, we would probably be the first thing they looked for, instead of going through all the drawers and cabinets in the kitchen and I assume Mom's hutch in the dining room."

"What do you think they want, Mariam?"

"Valuable stuff, probably. I've watched enough cop shows to know these guys usually know what they are looking for. If I were in their shoes, I would probably hit Mom and Dad's room next and look through Mom's jewelry case."

"But, we're upstairs, Mariam."

"Yeah, I know…that's the problem. We've gotta find a way to get downstairs and call the police. Heck, maybe we can hide in your room or something, since it's the closest to the staircase, and once they walk down the hall to Mom and Dad's room we can make a break for it."

"You really think that'll work?" Vince asked, clutching his stomach.

"I don't know, but… Hey, what's wrong?"

"My stomach. I think I gotta go."

"Can you hold it?"

"I don't think so…it really hurts."

Damn.

Even though Mariam had grown up in this house, she now wished that they lived in a newer home that had two bathrooms instead of just the one that was downstairs. She knew that not only would it be a risk to creep down the stairs without the two men seeing them, but then the sound of her brother's pee and other fluids splashing into the toilet would surely let the intruders know that someone else was inside the house. Crouching at the top of the stairs, she thought for a moment and then turned to her brother.

"I think I've got a cup in my room that I used this week for rinsing out my paint brushes, do you think you can go pee in that?"

"That's kinda gross," Vince replied, wrinkling his small nose.

Ugh.

"All right. Well, looks like we're gonna have to go downstairs now then."

"Yeah. We've gotta hurry, too. Not sure how much longer I can hold it."

"Okay. Let's go."

Mariam and Vince began to slowly descend the stairs. Mariam knew from sneaking out of the house late at night to meet her boyfriend, Bobby, that some of the steps squeaked, so they tried to avoid those. But she must have forgotten about one of them midway down the stairs, as the wood underneath the carpeted step groaned when she put her weight on it. She held her breath for a moment, waiting for the two men that were in the kitchen to race out and find them in the house. But they never did. She let the breath out as they continued down.

As they neared the bottom of the stairs, they could hear the men in the kitchen clinking beer bottles together and laughing about something. Mariam couldn't make out their words. The siblings made their way quickly and quietly off the stairs and headed down the hallway toward the bathroom.

About halfway down the hall, the house suddenly grew quiet. Mariam was afraid to look over her shoulder for fear of seeing the two men standing by the bottom of the stairs and looking at her and Vince creeping down the hallway. A moment later she heard one of the men laugh, telling her that they were still in the kitchen drinking their beers, and that it was okay for them to continue. A few long seconds later they were at the bathroom door. They pushed it open and rushed in. Mariam slowly closed the door and thumbed down the lock button on the doorknob. She didn't want to turn on the overhead light for fear of the men seeing it underneath the door, as she had done with Vince earlier in the night, so instead she moved the small switch on the night light beside the light switch to the on position. The glow of the small light filled the room, though she doubted anyone would be able to see it from underneath the door.

"Okay," Mariam whispered, "do what you have to do."

"With you in the room…that's kinda gross."

"Come on. We don't have a lot of time here. Tell ya what, I'll turn my back to you…how about that?"

"Yeah, okay. I guess that'll be all right."

It better be.

Vince pulled his shorts down and sat on the toilet seat. There was a small explosion into the water and then Mariam heard Vince urinating. She hoped the men that were (*still?*) in the kitchen couldn't hear it.

After a few minutes, Mariam heard her brother tear some toilet paper from the roll and wipe himself. *Thank God he's done*, Mariam thought, when suddenly a loud whooshing sound filled the room.

Oh no!

CHAPTER 10

WHEN JOHN AND Nick heard the toilet flush, they looked at each other for a second and then went running out of the kitchen. They were both out of breath by the time they reached the entranceway by the front door. They stopped and listened for movement. They heard none.

"Where's the bathroom, man?" Nick whispered.

"Not sure. But it can't be too hard to find…come on."

They started down the hallway in front of them. A door about ten feet ahead of the two men slowly opened, and a young boy peeked his head around the corner. Even through the darkness John could make out the whites of the boy's eyes. Then the boy was gone and the door slammed shut. The two men ran down the hall and started pounding on the bathroom door.

"Oh my God! What are we gonna do now?" Vince shrieked.

"You locked the door, right?" Mariam asked, pulling her brother close to her and sitting on the floor at the other end of the room.

"Yeah."

"Okay, good."

The men continued to pound on the door. Mariam thought she heard them laughing but wasn't sure.

"Mariam! What are we gonna do?"

Mariam wasn't sure what they were going to do now that the men had found out they were in the house. Before, she figured they had the advantage over the men, with the possibility of being able to sneak out of the house undetected, but not anymore. Especially now that the two men not only knew they were in the house, but knew exactly where they were: locked in the bathroom, with the men on the other side of the door trying to get in and do God knows what to both of them.

Mariam shook her head.

"What? Mariam! What?"

"I don't know."

"You don't know what?" Vince asked as tears started to form in his eyes and slowly run down both cheeks.

"I don't know...what we're gonna do. We're trapped."

After a few minutes, the two men stopped pounding.

"Shit, man. I think that little bitch saw my face," Nick said.

"Ah, don't worry about it, man."

"What do you mean, 'don't worry about it'? She *saw* me!"

"Like I said...don't worry about it. She'll never tell."

"Oh yeah? What makes you so sure?"

"'Cause...I won't let her have a chance to."

John put his finger up to his lips and then motioned for Nick to follow him.

Back into the kitchen.

CHAPTER 11

"WHAT YOU LOOKING for, man?" Nick asked as they entered the kitchen.

"Ah, you'll see. Something to keep those kids where they are…I saw something that I think will work in one of these drawers."

Nick followed John over to the kitchen counter and watched as he pulled open one drawer after the other.

After a few minutes, John pulled something that looked like rope out of a drawer and held it up for Nick to see.

"A rope?"

"Not quite. An extension cord…I figure it will work just as well."

"How the hell are we gonna tie them up if we can't even get in?" Nick asked.

"We're not going to tie them up, per se, but this'll keep them right where we want them…until we're ready for them."

Nick didn't quite know what John meant by "until we're ready for them," but figured he knew what he was doing. Nick knew John had done this type of job before, although he didn't know the details, and since this was Nick's first time robbing a house, he figured he would let John take the lead on what to do with the two kids. He followed John back out of the kitchen, through the dining room and down the hallway until they were standing outside the bathroom door again.

"So, what you gonna do?"

"Watch and ye shall see, my friend."

John proceeded to tie one end of the extension cord to the bathroom doorknob where the kids had locked themselves inside, and the other end he stretched across the hallway and fastened to the laundry room doorknob. He shook it a few times and then turned around to face Nick.

"Nice."

"Yeah, this should keep 'em right where we want 'em till we're ready."

Again with the "till we're ready" stuff, Nick said to himself as they walked out of the hallway and turned to go upstairs.

"Well, this must be one of the kids' rooms."

"Yup, looks like it all right…probably the little one."

"Yeah."

"But unless you want some stuffed animals or monster trucks, we probably won't find anything of value in here."

They walked out of the room and entered the one across the hallway. This one was darker than the last room they were in, as it didn't have a night light on. But, from the moon light coming in from the windows, Nick noticed that it must be the other girl's room, the older brother's.

"Hey, John."

"Yeah?"

"You think anything good will be in here?"

"Only one way to find out…you check the dresser and nightstand drawers, and I'll check out that desk over there."

"Cool."

John watched Nick walk over to the dresser and start looking through its drawers. He went over to the desk, sat down, and started looking through the various papers that were scattered here and there. He didn't find much. Bending over, he pulled out the top side drawer of the desk. He took his pen light from his pocket and thumbed down the button to turn it on. A small burst of light shot into the dark insides of the drawer, then bounced back at him.

Sitting in the back of the drawer was a small box with gold details etched on its top. It had a few small jewels as well, which John assumed were probably fake. It didn't matter though. He pulled it out, closed the drawer, and set the box on top of the desk.

"What'd you find?" Nick called from across the room.

"Don't know yet. But it could be good. Looks like the little shit tried to hide it pretty well. Come on over and check it out."

Nick abandoned the top drawer of the dresser, filled with panties and socks, and joined John at the desk.

John opened the box and shined his light in. He almost shrieked for joy upon seeing what was inside.

"Damn," is all Nick could say.

"Yup. Jackpot!"

Inside the box were several rings, bracelets, and necklaces. Even though they were old looking and tarnished, John could tell they were antiques and were probably family heirlooms passed down from generation to generation. He reached in and selected one of the rings to get a closer look.

"Man, look at this," John said, almost drooling over the thing.

"How much you think it's worth?"

"Man, I don't know. A black diamond ring like this...who knows...big bucks probably."

"Nice."

"Yeah, no shit nice! We should be able to fetch a pretty penny for this thing."

John motioned for Nick to open the bag they had brought upstairs with them, which contained the loot from the kitchen and dining room, and threw it in.

"I don't know about some of this stuff...but most of this is the real McCoy."

"Might as well take it all and sort through it later."

"Now you're learning, buddy," John said as he picked up the gold box and dumped the remaining contents into the bag. Then he threw in the box for good measure. "Not sure if that box is real gold or not...but like my momma used to say, 'better safe than sorry.'"

"Your momma sounds like a smart woman."

"Darn tootin'."

They searched the rest of the older sister's room but didn't find anything else. They returned to the hallway, turned left, and started walking toward the master bedroom. That's when they heard a crash and froze in their tracks.

CHAPTER 12

MARIAM STOOD BACK as the bathroom window shattered. She knew the sound of the breaking glass would probably be loud enough for the two men to hear no matter where they were in the house. If they were *still* inside the house. Mariam figured they were, probably going through her stuff in her bedroom by now, which made her even more angry about the situation. She hated it when her little brother or her parents would go snooping around in her business. She was old enough now to deserve some privacy, but it rarely went that way. Especially not with her mother's way of thinking that she was always trying to hide something just because she was a teenager. The truth of the matter was, she really didn't have much to hide. Unless you count her diary, tucked away and hidden inside her top desk drawer, that told in sometimes great deal when her and her boyfriend, Bobby, had sex, and if they had used protection or not. She had even jotted down when he came inside her. It had only happened a couple times since they had started doing it a few months ago, and she had thought it was hot when it happened, but afterwards she always felt guilty. Not guilty that she was sharing herself with Bobby or even letting him come inside her. No, it was because she had always told her mom that if she ever did have intercourse, she would be careful and use protection and never come home one night and say she was pregnant. Fortunately, she had never gotten pregnant, though she thought she could have been a few times. She never even told her mom that she and Bobby were having sex. Mariam figured it was her personal business, no one else's. She had always kept that she was having sex from everyone, including her friends, but now that the two men had probably found her diary and looked through it and saw that she was sexually active, she had the distinct fear that now everyone would know: her parents, brother, friends, the school, the local newspaper, TV news, everyone. Mariam knew the idea of that actually happening was unlikely, but she was afraid of it all the same. That was one of the reasons she had broken out the bathroom window. Not only because they couldn't get the door open, not only because she was responsible for protecting her brother, but also because she knew that two strange men were going through her personal property. In the grand scheme of things, it mattered little if everyone found out that she was having sex with her boyfriend, but it bothered her all the same and she knew, in that instant, that she not only had to find a phone to call the cops, but she also needed to get back to her room and retrieve her diary. She knew her rationalization was weak, but she didn't know how else to think.

She stepped back from the window another foot or so and turned to her brother. "Okay, Vince. Here's the plan. I'm going to go out first. Once I get out there and down to the ground, you climb up on the toilet and shimmy yourself out the window and I'll catch you from below."

"Don't you think it would be better if I go first?"

"I thought about that, but no. It's at least a ten-foot drop from the window to the ground, and I don't want you busting an ankle or something when you land."

"I can make it."

"I don't really want to take that chance, ya know? Especially not since I am responsible for you. I don't want Mom and Dad to blame me for you getting hurt."

"Getting *hurt* is a lot better than what happened to poor Dr. Blythworth."

"Yeah, that's true. But still. I really think it's better for me to go first and be out there to catch you."

"All right. Whatever you say."

"But before I climb out, I need a towel."

"A towel...what for? You're not wet."

"No, I'm not. But I need something to put across the bottom of the window frame so I don't get all gashed up by the broken glass."

"Oh, okay. Good thinking...I'll get one for you."

Vince walked over, opened up the linen closet, and pulled out a giant, white cotton towel. Mariam took it from him and draped it over the bottom of the window frame. As she patted it into place, she could feel some of the broken glass that was still embedded in the frame, but the towel seemed thick enough so that the glass wouldn't cut through and slice her up on her way out the window. She climbed up onto the toilet.

"All right, here goes," Mariam said, kicking one foot onto the window frame.

That's when she heard something on the other side of the bathroom door.

As she shimmied her way out the window and was about ready to jump to the ground, the bathroom door suddenly exploded open and the two men rushed in.

She fell.

Out the window.

CHAPTER 13

MARIAM HIT THE ground with her feet, hard, did a somersault, and stood up. As she brushed grass and dirt off the backside of her shorts, she looked up and saw her brother trying to get through the window. His head was hanging out. His arms were flailing up and down. He was screaming, "Mariam! No, please! Don't touch me! MOM!" and then he was gone.

"You dirty bastards! Let my brother go!" Mariam screamed up at the window.

Mariam heard the two men laughing and then one of them poked his head out the broken window. It was too dark to make out what he looked like. Though Mariam could tell the man had long hair and the slight breeze was blowing it into his face. He screamed down at her.

"Here…little…piggy…piggy…piggy…"

"Go to hell!" Mariam screamed up at him.

"Oh, what a voice on such a cute little girl," the man said.

The way the man said it made gooseflesh crawl all over her skin.

"You better be a good little girl," the man said, "or I'll gut your brother like a fish."

"You'll do no such thing!"

"Oh, you'd be surprised what I'm capable of if I don't get what I want. The stuff in your parents' house is only part of why we picked this place…the other stuff…well…your brother will find out soon enough," he said, laughing, and then he was gone.

Mariam could hear Vince inside the house pleading with the two men to stop touching him, to let him go, but they were obviously not going to do so, no matter what he said. Mariam knew that it was up to her to save her brother, to protect him, just as she had promised her parents she would do. Even though she or her parents had never dreamed that something like this would happen, she still knew that even if she had to risk life or limb, she had to save her brother. Besides, even though Vince bothered the hell out of her most of the time, she loved the little shit and didn't want to see anything bad happen to him.

She took off and ran to the back of the house.

* * *

When she rounded and came to the back of the house, she noticed that one of the windows on the back door had been broken out. She assumed this was how the two men had gained entrance. She knew that no matter how many guard-chains or dead-bolts her parents had installed on the door, it wouldn't have made any difference. The two men had simply broken out a pane of glass, reached in, and unlocked the door. So the house is easy to break into, Mariam thought. It still doesn't explain why they picked *our* house. Unless they knew Mom and Dad would be away for the weekend. This means they were probably watching when Mom and Dad pulled away in the car and just waited until dark to break in. *Damn!* This definitely means they killed Dr. Blythworth at the front door. *Ugh!* Mariam had seen enough cop shows to know how it worked.

She quietly walked up to the back door, pushed it open and looked inside. She couldn't see or hear the two men or her brother anywhere. She carefully reached in and picked up the phone off its base, quickly punched in three numbers, and stretched the cord so that she could lean up against the house, out of sight of the two men if they should wander back into the kitchen.

She put the phone up to her ear, waiting for the 911 operator to pick up and ask, "911…what is your emergency?" but it never came. In fact, she didn't hear anything at all coming from the phone. There was no purring sound indicating that a phone was ringing on the other end of the line, or anything else for that matter. She peeked around the corner of the door and, not seeing anyone, quickly hung the phone up, picked it up again, and tapped in the same three numbers. She put the phone up to her ear again. Nothing. What the hell, Mariam thought, as she repeated the process of hanging up the phone and picking it back up once more. This time she didn't dial 911. Instead, she put the receiver up to her ear and listened for a dial tone. There was none. The two men must have cut the phone line on the outside of the house.

Damn!

She reached her arm inside and quietly put the phone back on its base. She still didn't hear any sounds coming from inside.

She leaned back up against the side of the house and sighed.

She had no idea what to do next.

CHAPTER 14

AFTER CLAMPING A hand over the boy's mouth, John pulled him, kicking and screaming, from the bathroom into the hallway. He knew that the first order of business was to tie up the little pipsqueak and then find the older one, wherever she had run off to. He knew deep down that the older one would never totally abandon her brother, so she had to be around the house somewhere. Probably hiding in the bushes or something, he thought, nodding to Nick to pick up the boy's feet and help him carry him upstairs.

A short while later they were at the top of the stairs. Without removing his hand from the boy's mouth, he asked him which room was his. He nodded and looked to his right. Just as they had thought when searching the rooms the first time. They carried him in and laid him down on the bed.

"Nick. Go in his closet and find something to tie him up with."

"Okay."

After searching for a few minutes, Nick held up a pair of old shoes. Their laces were untied and dangling from their eyes. "How's this?" he asked.

"That'll work. Find another pair, too. We'll use one shoelace for each of his arms and legs and tie them to the bedposts...he won't be going anywhere then."

"Nice."

After finding another pair of shoes, Nick removed all the laces and handed two of them to John. John set to tying the boy's wrists to the bedposts, while Nick worked on his ankles. John picked up a dirty sock that was lying on the floor and stuffed it in the boy's mouth. "That'll keep him from yappin',"" he said as he pulled up the boy's left arm and tied it off.

When all the boy's limbs were tied off and the sock in his mouth was secure, John nodded to Nick, turned off the night light, and walked out of the room, shutting the door behind them.

"That should keep him from getting away."

"Yeah...but, what in the hell are we gonna do with him?" Nick asked.

"Hummm...well...that's a good question, my dear Watson...hummm...actually, we can do whatever we want with him. We can kill him outright *or* we can have some fun with him first...maybe cut him a little...see how much he screams...there's a ton of possibilities with something like this."

"You're sick, you know that?"

"Yup. Proud of it, too."

They started down the hall toward the stairs.

"One question, though," Nick began. "Why do we have to kill him at all? I mean, shit, he looks scared half to death, ya know. It's not like he'll say anything to anybody."

"Hey, you're the one that was just bitchin' a while ago about him seeing your face and shit. Now you wanna just let him live? Fuck that. That little shit is gonna die a slow death if I have anything to say about it. But first...we gotta find his older sister and secure her. Then it'll be time to search the rest of this motha and see what else we can score."

"Yeah...okay...I guess you're right."

"Damn straight I'm right. Listen, I've done this dozens of times. The one thing my mentor taught me, what I want to pass down to you, is that you never leave someone alive that might be able to identify you. Hell, you don't start doing shit like that, no matter if you think they're too scared to tell on you or not, you just don't take that chance."

"Yeah. Okay. So what's next? How do we find his sister?" Nick asked, walking behind John down the stairs.

"Well, the way I see it...she'll be somewhere around the house still, ya know? Maybe not inside, but she'll be around. Maybe hiding out in the garage or behind some bushes in the back yard or something. I know one thing for sure."

"What's that?"

"A sibling is never going to leave the other one to die. And I imagine from the older one seeing how we did the dude on the porch earlier, she's not going to take the chance to venture far from the house to call the cops. 'Cause if you think about it, in her mind we're probably killing her brother right now, or at least talking about how to do it. And if I were her, I wouldn't want to take that chance, ya know?"

"Yeah…guess that does make some sense."

"Hell yes, it makes perfect sense…now come on."

* * *

Mariam was still hiding just outside the back door when she heard the two men enter the kitchen. She squatted down to the ground and held her breath.

Even though she was fairly close, she couldn't make out everything that was being said. But from what she could decipher, they were talking about her brother, something about killing him, and something about finding *her* first before robbing the rest of the place. It sounded like both her and her brother were in a boat, floating upon an ocean of shit, without a paddle.

As the two men continued to discuss where to look for *her* first, Mariam started to think about what she needed to do next. Her first order of business had been to call the police. But now that the phone line was dead, she didn't see how that was possible. She thought about running to a neighbor's house and seeing if they were awake and asking them if she could use their phone. But going to a neighbor's house would mean leaving her brother behind. She didn't like that idea at all. Secondly, she didn't know, if she *did* try to run to a neighbor's house, that the two men weren't watching for her out a window. If they were, they would surely see her streaking across the lawn and would probably start running after her. Mariam knew that she was fast for her age, she ran the 100m in track, but more than likely wasn't faster than two grown men, so she didn't want to go that route, either. The only thing that seemed to make sense at this juncture was to think of some way to enter the house without the two men knowing about it, find Vince, wherever they had taken him, and then both of them making a run for it. Besides, if it were both of them, at least the odds would be a little fairer. Well, Mariam thought, not totally fair, we would be just two kids against two grown men, but it would be better than one against two.

Think, Mariam…think, damnit!

CHAPTER 15

"ALL RIGHT, THIS is what we'll do," John began, grabbing Nick's now-warm beer off the counter and handing it to him. Nick took a sip. His face scrunched up when he tasted it. It was warm, but he swallowed it anyway.

"We'll split up and search for the little bitch."

"Sounds simple enough."

"Yeah, it does. But remember, if you don't know your opponent, things can turn sour in a hurry."

"Come on, John. What is the girl, fifteen...seventeen at the most...how hard can it be?"

"You'd be surprised. Just keep your wits about you when we split up. If you have the chance to bag her, do it. But if she has some sort of weapon, call me and I'll come runnin'."

"Come runnin' with what?"

"This," John said, pulling the closed straight razor out of his pocket and flipping it open to reveal a long, shiny blade.

"Nice."

"You damn right, buddy. This thing here was my mentor's blade."

"I thought you told me once that he was taken down by the cops."

"Oh, yeah, he was, all right. But...I have a buddy that works for the fuzz and he was able to get it outta the evidence room for me."

"Nice. It's cool and all that you have a blade, but don't you think it would be a good idea if I carry something as well?"

"Yeah, probably not a bad idea at all...choose your poison," John said, pointing to a large butcher rack filled with knives.

"Ohhh...preeety." Nick laughed and then selected the longest one in the rack, the butcher knife. He drew it out, moved it up to his face and twisted it from side to side. The moonlight coming in through the window glinted off the blade. "Yeah, I think this will work just fine."

"Good. Now, let's get to it. You take the house and I'll search the yard and garage."

* * *

Hearing the two men talk about searching for her and razors and knives sent a chill up Mariam's spine. She knew that she had to get back in the house to save her brother, but was scared to death. She had never had a close encounter with death and surely didn't want now to be the time. She also knew, though, that she didn't really have a choice. If she was going to save Vince and do it in a timely fashion, rather than go around and see what neighbors *might* still be awake at this ungodly hour, she had to decide what her next move was going to be. Getting back into the house was the first mission. Then she had to creep around, trying not to make any noise so that the man called Nick wouldn't find her and cut her up before she could find Vince. Then, finally, there would be the trouble of escaping the house. She thought for a second. Yeah, that should be it. Just go inside, find Vince, and vamoose from the place. Easy. But in her gut, Mariam knew it wouldn't be easy. Then another thought popped into her head.

Shit! After we escape, if we're even able to...then what?

She knew that after they made it from the house they would have to either hide or start going around knocking on their neighbors' doors, hoping one of them would wake up, answer the door, not freak out about them being on their porch so late at night, and let them inside. Just the thought of escaping from the house and then not being able to find a place to hide in time before the two men spotted them and started chasing made her gut drop. She wanted to bend over and puke, but she knew she didn't have time for such luxury. After taking a few deep breaths and saying to herself, *Okay, Mariam, just take it one step at a time*, she pushed herself up and made her way to the front of the house.

If those bastards get to have weapons, so do I, she said to herself, thinking about finding something sharp for protection amidst all her father's wood-working tools.

Luckily, she found the side door to the garage unlocked. She figured the gods must be looking down upon her because her father normally kept it locked. He was a stickler about his tools and normally locked the door whether he was home or not. He especially never left it unlocked when both he and her mom went away for a weekend. Mariam also knew that the garage was strictly off-limits, per the rules of the house, which she thought was silly, but did understand since there were a lot of tools worth a lot of money that her father used for his side-business of making stools, armchairs, shelves, benches and the like for folks around town.

Mariam pushed the door open and entered the dark confines of the garage. Even though she was well aware of where her father's bench saw, grinder, drill press, and other large equipment was, she knew she wouldn't be able to use any of those as a weapon to protect herself; she would need to search the workbench for a handheld tool, so she flipped the garage light on. The burst of light from the fluorescent bulbs blinded her at first, but then her eyes adjusted. She walked by several machines and came upon the workbench. As always, it was in impeccable condition, without a scrap of wood or sawdust to be found.

After searching through her father's tools, she ended up selecting a small, handheld power drill and a large claw hammer. She stuck each of them into a rear pocket of her khaki shorts.

She turned around and headed for the door.

Before she could reach it, the door flew open.

A long-haired man carrying a straight razor stepped inside the garage. He reached over and flicked down the light switch.

The room went black.

She screamed.

CHAPTER 16

EVEN THOUGH HE was inside the house and tied down to the bed, Vince could hear the scream. He could tell it came from somewhere outside the house, and he knew it was his sister. Knowing that at least one of the two men had caught Mariam made a lump form in his throat. He began to cry. The tears rolled off his cheeks, hitting the pillow his head was resting on. Snot bubbles popped outside his nose. He felt like he was going to throw up. He choked down the rising bile in his throat.

Not knowing if his sister was still alive, Vince started to think about all the good times he had had with Mariam. The times they played ball in the back yard, kickball at the park, or hopscotch in the front driveway were all still fresh in his mind like they happened yesterday. He now wished that he hadn't been such a brat to his older sister. He wished that he had been more loving and let his sister know just how much she truly meant to him. He hoped Mariam knew all this. But Vince feared that she didn't. The thought of his sister dying by the hands of one of the two men that had tied him to the bed made him sick to his stomach. Vince wished it was him being hurt by the two men instead of Mariam. He knew in that instant that if they had given him the option of who would die tonight, he would have told them to pick him instead of his sister. He loved Mariam that much.

He began to cry even harder.

With the sock stuffed in his mouth, it was difficult to breathe.

His body began shaking uncontrollably.

He was more pissed than anything else.

He had to find a way to escape and help his sister.

If she was even still alive.

Vince knew that he would never forgive himself if he didn't at least try to help Mariam.

He started to jerk his arms and legs this way and that, trying to free himself.

After a while, the knot that had been made in the shoelace which held his right wrist to the bedpost began to loosen.

* * *

Nick was searching for the girl in the living room when he heard the scream. He took off running. As he neared the front door, he thought about using that to go outside, but then thought better of it. It would be his luck that if he did that, someone would be driving by in their car or walking their dog on the front sidewalk and see him bolting out of the house carrying a large knife. If that happened, they would surely call the cops on their cell phone, and if they weren't carrying a cell phone, Nick figured it would be a neighbor of the house they had been robbing, and they would be close enough to *their* house to get home, pick up the phone, and call the cops. Either way, if someone saw him running out the front door it would bring nothing but trouble for him and John. He didn't need that. He also knew damn well that John would probably kill him while they were in jail if they were caught on the job.

He took off running toward the back door instead.

With his first step into the kitchen his foot slipped under him. As his legs began going this way and that, and his arms started to pinwheel through the air, he realized that he must have gotten some blood from the dead doctor on his shoes when he ran past the front door. He thought he was going to fall, but was able to keep his forward momentum going enough so that it didn't happen. He was glad about that. He didn't want to look like a horse's ass on his first day on the job.

He staggered out the back door and started running. He wasn't exactly sure where the scream had come from, but he figured it came from the garage.

Arms and legs pumping, he held the large butcher knife tight in his right hand, ready for whatever lay ahead.

CHAPTER 17

THE GARAGE WAS pitch black. Mariam raised her hand and waved it in front of her face, hoping that she would at least be able to see something so close to her. But she couldn't. She could hear the muffled breathing of the long-haired man somewhere in the garage, but couldn't see him. She knew that if she could hear his breathing he was probably close, but more than likely wasn't close enough to get her yet. If he was, Mariam figured he would have probably already tried to reach out and grab her and then do God knows what to her. She really didn't want him to get her, but also didn't know what to do because of how dark the room was. Trying to ignore the man in the room, she began to shuffle her feet forward and reached her arms in front of her body. She felt like she was the character Jodie Foster played in *Silence of the Lambs*, when she was down in the crazy man's basement; it was dark as hell, and she was trying to find out where he was hiding. But this time, it wasn't Jodie Foster trying to find a serial killer, it was Mariam trying to find a hiding place or a way to escape so the psycho bastard that was inside the garage wouldn't find her.

She continued to inch her way forward.

As she moved through the garage, Mariam tried to keep some of her senses on the man's breathing and his approximate location, and not on the fear building inside her guts of what would happen if he did find her.

Something brushed against her forehead and she screamed. She then felt the tight grip of arms wrapping around her arms and chest. With her lungs still empty from the scream, she wasn't able to suck in any more oxygen. She felt like her face was turning purple and her head was going to explode. As the man clutched her against his chest, Mariam could feel wisps of his long hair brushing against the side of her face. He smelled of cigarette smoke and impending doom. The thoughts of never seeing her mother and father again began to race through her mind. Even though her parents were strict the majority of the time and it gave Mariam headaches when trying to stay out with her friends after curfew, she knew that her parents were really only trying to do what was best for her. She knew they loved her and cared for her very much. Mariam now wished that she hadn't been such a moody teenager and had given her parents the benefit of the doubt more times than she had. But now, she knew it was too late. She wasn't going to be able to see them again, tell them how sorry she was for being such a little shit through the last few years, and let them know how much *she* loved them. The next thing that popped into Mariam's head was her brother, Vince. In addition to being a nicer person to her parents, she now wished that she had been a better big sister to Vince. The little squirt wasn't all that bad to hang out with, but more times than not Mariam had acted like he was being a nuisance and told him to get out of her room and leave her alone. As the man's long hair continued to brush against her face, she wished she had been a better sister and showed Vince "the ropes" of being a kid, so to speak.

Her rump hit the floor.

She figured that the man had let go of her and let her drop onto the floor, as she was now able to suck air into her aching lungs. She coughed. Bringing her hand down from covering her mouth, she could feel something sticky on her fingers. Hoping it wasn't some of the man's saliva, she brought it back up to her face and gave it a sniff. It didn't smell of stale cigarette smoke like she had figured it would. Instead, her fingers smelled of dust and stale air.

What the…

The man's breathing continued to fill the dark garage.

* * *

As Nick ran through the back yard, he heard the second scream and picked up his pace. He figured that John had already gotten the girl, or she had just screamed again after seeing the straight razor. *She's probably pissing her pretty little panties by now*, Nick thought, almost to the corner of the house. He could see the side door of the garage only thirty or so feet ahead and off to the right.

Mmmm...I bet she's one of those teeny boppers that likes to wear those boy-short panties and drive all the guys crazy in her class when she bends over to pick something up off the floor and the top of her panties show above her shorts...

Nick could feel the strain of his penis against the inside of his pants as he turned the corner of the house.

Maybe John will let me...

The back side of a shovel crashed against his face and he crumbled to the ground.

CHAPTER 18

WHEN MARIAM REALIZED that it had been cobwebs and not the man's long hair brushing against her forehead and face, she wanted to laugh at how stupid she had been. Not only because they were only cobwebs on her face and hands, but because she had been dumb enough to scream and give her exact location to the long-haired man.

As she pushed herself off the floor and brushed off her hands and the back of her shorts, she still didn't understand how she felt someone's arms wrapping around her when clearly there hadn't been any. The only conclusion she could come up with was that, since she had thought the cobwebs were the man's breath and hair, her mind had run away from her after the fact. This, of course, didn't make her feel any better. Actually, it made her feel like a horse's ass, but she knew that she didn't have much time to feel that way about herself, because the man was coming—she could tell from his breathing—getting closer and closer.

She started to inch her way through the darkness again. She heard him laugh and wanted to puke from the sound of it.

"Here, little piggy, piggy, piggy...come out, come out, come out...wherever you are," the man whispered, laughing in between each word.

"Shut up!" Mariam shouted.

"Ah, come on now. I promise I won't hurt you."

"Yeah, right. I think I've heard that line in a movie or two, buster."

Mariam really didn't want to continue bantering with the man, but she didn't have much choice—she was pissed. Pissed at him and his buddy for killing Dr. Blythworth, pissed about them breaking into her family's house, and pissed about them chasing her and Vince around like a couple of rats stuck in a cage, and she wanted to let him know that she wasn't happy with the situation.

"Seriously. Why in the world are you doing this?" Mariam asked, continuing to search the darkness in front of her with her arms. Her left shin banged against one of her father's standing wood-working benches and it hurt like a son of a bitch. She wanted to scream, shout, cry out and grab her throbbing leg, but she knew if she did that it would mean she would have to stop walking. If she stopped walking and continued to chat with the long-haired man, she knew that he would be able to find her a lot easier than if she kept moving. So she ignored the growing welt on her leg and kept moving.

As she continued through the dark, she thought about how large her father's garage really was. Sure, she had been inside before, but it had always been during the daytime, with her father, and it was normally just for a moment or two; to tell him dinner was ready or to grab the car-care bucket for cleaning up the inside and out of her parents' Mercedes. During those few times in the garage, she had never more than quickly scanned the area. But now, moving around in the dark garage, she realized how massive the thing was. She also realized that even though the main door had windows, the door that would be manually (*damn old house, again*) lifted for a car to drive through if her father hadn't converted the area into a workshop, there was barely any light coming in from the moon. Mariam thought that was strange, but also knew it was no time for an astronomy lesson with an emphasis on lunar movement. She was about ready to laugh at herself for thinking such a silly thing when the man's heavy breathing (*damn smokers killing themselves with those cancer sticks*) started again. Then he spoke.

"Ah, come on now. You're not mad at me…are you?" Mariam heard the question loud and clear. She also heard the man stifle a chuckle after saying it.

"You *are* a real prick, ya know that, mister…" Mariam paused.

"Just call me John."

"Okay. John."

"And your name is, my dear?"

"Mariam."

"Ohhh…what a pretty name for a pretty little piggy," John said, then began laughing. Mariam might have laughed as well if the man standing in the dark garage with her wasn't trying to do God only knows what to her and her brother.

If Vince is even still alive, that is…

Mariam wanted to punch herself for thinking such a thing, but knew that it might be true. For all she knew, right now, Vince was lying in his own pool of blood similar to Dr. Blythworth. She also knew that if her brother was indeed hurt or dead, there would be hell to pay from her parents, even if it hadn't been her fault. She had been put in charge of looking out for the house and Vince, and not only was her brother possibly dead but the house was going to be burglarized, all her parents' stuff taken, her father's wood-working equipment would be stolen, and…

She reached her hand around and pulled out one of her father's tools from the rear pocket of her khaki shorts.

The handheld power drill.

Then Mariam *did* laugh.

At what the fate of the long-haired man would be if he tried to mess with her.

CHAPTER 19

ROBERT LOOKED OVER at his wife and could tell she was nervous and scared. Hell, he was too. Well, that and a little pissed off about being disturbed by the front desk clerk when he rang their hotel room. They had only been asleep for thirty minutes or so before the call came through. A few minutes after that, they were dressed, out of the hotel and into the Mercedes. That was about thirty minutes ago.

It wasn't that he didn't love his children very much, but he had been working hard over the past several weeks so that he and Julia could take a long weekend, drive into the city, stay at a posh hotel, have a fabulous dinner, have lots of drinks and cap the night off by making love…several times. Which they had done. The whole night had been fabulous until the call.

Now they were racing home, all because of some strange message someone had left for them via the hotel's main telephone number. Even though the message had been conveyed in that fashion, rather than talking with him or his wife directly, it was still enough to scare the everliving shit out of them both; enough to make it a somewhat easy decision to call the weekend quits after only one night in the city.

Robert pressed down on the accelerator and whipped past an old lady doing 50 in a 70 mile per hour zone. For good measure, he blared his horn on the way by. He looked over at Julia, who was giving him a dirty look, even with tears streaming down her cheeks. He was going to say something to her, as he always hated it when someone was a "backseat driver" when he was behind the wheel, but given the circumstances he bit his tongue and instead reached over and stroked the back of her neck. She turned her head toward him. Her words came out in a whisper of sobs.

"Robby, do you really think the kids are in trouble?" she asked.

Choking back the last remnants of anger from earlier at the hotel, he said, "I don't know, Julia. I really don't. But that message was definitely strange enough to raise some doubts inside me that they might not be okay."

"Oh my God…what are we gonna do?"

"I don't know, sweetheart. I really don't."

"So, tell me again… What was it that the front desk clerk said to you?"

"I already told you, Julia," he replied, zipping around another slow-moving car on the interstate.

"Yes, I know that, Robert! But, just for my sake…please tell me again."

Robert sighed and then said, "Okay."

"Well, from what the front desk said," Robert began, "a neighbor of ours, of course he didn't say who, happened to look out their window and saw a sedan pull into our driveway. The person didn't think much of it at the time, figured it was one of Mariam's friends or something, and went back to the television program they had been watching. A short time later, when the person got up from their chair to fetch a drink in the kitchen, they decided to take another look out their window. When they did, that is when they saw what happened."

"Which was?"

"Come on, Julia. I already told you this. If I tell you again, all you'll do is get yourself all worked up and we don't need that right now… Hell, I don't need that right now."

"Jesus, Robert! Why do you have to be so rude all the time?"

"Hey!" he shouted. "You weren't saying I was rude just a short time ago when my dick was in your—"

"Okay, enough. Enough. I get it. But, please…"

"All right. Damn. I'll tell you, but you better not get upset again."

"I'll try."

Robert took a deep breath and finished telling the story to Julia. He explained how their neighbor, after getting a drink from the kitchen and looking out their window, saw Mariam open the door and someone proceeded to fall onto her. He also explained how the neighbor didn't see the body moving and presumed the person was either unconscious or dead. His wife started crying again when he finished.

"So…" Julia said, choking back a flood of tears, "why didn't our neighbor, whoever the hell it was, call the police after seeing something like that?"

"Hell if I know, dear. Maybe he or she thought that it wasn't real, ya know? Maybe they thought it was one of Mariam's friends playing a joke and didn't want to get the police involved over a stupid teenager-type prank. Shit, I really don't know that to think. But one thing I do know is that someone better be dead when we get home or someone is gonna end up that way, and…"

"Robert Michael Oster!"

"Christ! What?"

"How could you say such a thing! They're *your* kids, for Christ's sake. What if they're really in trouble or hurt or one of them is…"

"Now, now…" Robert said, reaching behind Julia and stroking her neck again. As he was doing it, he really did start to feel like shit. Sure, he was Vince's *real* father and Mariam was only his step-daughter, and he knew he should feel about them and treat them the same, but it was hard to do sometimes. Especially when Mariam was up to her old teenager-type stuff: sneaking out of the house late at night, trying to get curfew extended by calling five minutes before she ought to be home and saying, "Sorry, Dad, I just lost track of time, ya know? Would it be okay if I stay over at Samantha's house a little while longer? I mean, if I leave now, I'll still be late, ya know, so I might as well just stay another half hour or hour or…and finish up our homework." He did honestly love it that she called him "Dad," though. Hell, her real father up and left Julia out of the blue in the middle of the night, so he knew he should give the kid some leeway, but it still pissed him off all the same that something always came up with her. Having to pick her up from here, drop her off there, pay this, pay that…it was an expensive endeavor having a teenager in the house.

Hell, it wasn't even his plan to have a kid until he met Julia. Well, he wasn't even thinking about children at all—just the art of what it took to make one. All he saw when he met her in that bar so many years ago was a sweet young thing, no older than 42 or so, with long legs, long blonde hair, and an ass that made his dick go hard just by looking at it. He had known that very night, when he first saw her and a group of friends (he would later learn it was a party for Julia to celebrate her freedom from that bastard of a husband that had left her) walk into that bar. From that point, all he had to do was buy her a few drinks, talk the talk, and a few hours later they were in a hotel room together, kissing, fondling, sucking, licking, and fucking each other over and over again. Just thinking about it now made Robert's hackles turn blue, aching for release. But then he thought about how he had received a call from Julia a few months after their one night stand, telling him that she was pregnant, and no, she hadn't been with anyone else, and yes, it was his. At the time he didn't want to believe it and demanded a DNA test, which was performed via amniocentesis. When the results came back, yes, he was indeed the father. After that happened, they ended up talking on the phone now and again, trying to think of a way to handle the situation. Eventually, they started going out to dinner…then fell in love with one another…and finally they wed when Julia was 7 ½ months pregnant.

Robert looked over at Julia, who was still crying, and truly *did* feel like a horse's ass for not being more sympathetic to her feelings. He knew, in his heart, that he did love Mariam and Vince and her and it had just been his immaturity as a man, even in his early fifties now, that he had felt some sort of anger back in the hotel room. The truth of the matter was that he did sincerely hope that the kids were okay and that the message that had been left for them at the hotel was just a big misunderstanding.

He gave his wife's neck a gentle squeeze and pressed down on the accelerator again.

They would be home in less than an hour.

He hoped the kids would still be okay when they finally got there.

CHAPTER 20

VINCE STARTED TO work on the knot holding his right ankle against the bed frame. After what seemed like an hour, but was no more than a few minutes, he gave up and collapsed back onto the bed. Sweat poured down his face and neck. It soaked into the pillow his head had been lying on. It smelled of body odor and sick. He felt like shit. His head was pounding. His stomach was cramping. He needed an aspirin and to use the bathroom. If he wasn't able to get out of the bed and run downstairs soon and into the bathroom, he felt like he would soil himself.

Great, that's all I need. First I'm sick and Mariam has to take care of me like I'm some old person that can't do anything for themselves, and now I'm going to poop my pants like some little ankle biter. Yeah, Mom and Dad will really *let me stay home alone with Mariam again.*

Vince didn't want that to happen.

Up until he had come down with a case of the runs, he and Mariam had been having a grand time playing video games and a board game and were about to make some popcorn and watch a scary movie. Vince didn't care all that much for those types of films, but since Mariam was into them, he figured it was the least he could do. He felt a little bad about Mariam having to watch him for the whole weekend and not be able to go out with her boyfriend. On the other hand, Mariam did talk her parents into letting her stay home and take care of things, so Vince supposed that his sister couldn't have cared all that much about not being able to go out with Bobby. Though he did hear them on the phone earlier in the night, talking about seeing each other "later," and figured that he was going to sneak into the house after he had fallen asleep and creep up into Mariam's room.

Shaking the thoughts of his sister and some guy rolling around in bed together, naked, sweating, and grunting up a storm, Vince sat his wary body up and started picking at the knot again.

The fate of his sister and his clean shorts hung in the balance.

* * *

Mariam could tell the long-haired man was getting closer now. Even in the dark she could feel his presence. His breathing was now rapid and huffy. The hairs on the back of her neck stood on end. Her bowels tightened. She really didn't want to think about what he would do to her if he caught her, but it was hard not to let the negative thoughts run a marathon through her mind. She pictured the man coming up from behind her, wrapping his arms around her and squeezing. The breath would gush out of her. Her head would feel like it was about to explode from the lack of oxygen. Finally it would happen. She would pass out. Mariam pictured him lying her on the floor, tearing off her blouse and shorts with his hands, before removing her bra and panties with his teeth. Then his dirty hands would be all over her.

This fucker tries any of that shit with me, I'll drill his eye out with this thing.

The man's breathing sounded closer now.

Mariam started to move again. Cobwebs brushed through her hair, and something bounced off her forehead. She almost screamed again until she realized what it was.

A golf ball. The ball had been fashioned by her father to a rope which led up to the attic above the garage.

YES!

She reached up to grab the rope, but at the same time a pair of hands grabbed her and she was pulled away from her temporary escape from the long-haired man.

She wanted to scream, but only a whimper came out.

She *knew* what was in store for her.

CHAPTER 21

ROBERT LOOKED DOWN at the dash of the Mercedes. The green numbers told him that they still had forty-five minutes until they would be home. He looked over at his wife, who was also staring at the time. They had been silent for some time now and even though he wasn't exactly sure what to say to her to calm her fears of what lay ahead at the house, he knew he had to say something.

"Honey, how are you doing?"

"How the hell do you think I am doing, Robert? Our kids are in trouble, well, let's just hope they are still in trouble and not dead or something, and we still have a long way to go until we're home."

Robert looked down at the clock again. Only two minutes had passed since he had last checked.

"They'll be okay, Julia."

"How can you be so sure?"

"Because I have faith that Mariam can take care of the house or I wouldn't have agreed that she could stay there alone. Besides, for all we know, our *neighbor* that supposedly saw whatever they think they saw could have the whole thing blown out of proportion. Like we talked about before, it could just be Bobby or one of Mariam's girlfriends that stopped by and was playing a practical joke."

"Yeah, I guess. But what if they *are* in trouble?"

Robert thought for a moment and then he had an idea.

"Well, I suppose I could call Bill across the street and have him go over and check on the kids."

"Yeah! Why the hell didn't you think about that before?"

"Because, I know how the kids, or at least Mariam, feel about him. She would never forgive us if nothing is wrong and I have Bill go over and knock on the door and ask if everything is okay. Shit. The hell with forgiving us, she'd never let me forget it. She'd be on my ass like white on rice, for heaven's sakes."

"You have a point there."

"Besides, like I said, I'm sure that everything is fine. Whoever left that message for us at the hotel probably didn't see all of what happened."

"What do you mean?"

"Well, he or she said that a body fell on the front porch and wasn't moving. Then they went and called the hotel we were staying at. Shit. Now I wish we hadn't given the number to so many damn people on the block or we'd be able to narrow it down to who actually called."

"Hey, that was your idea, not mine. You're the one that said before we left that leaving the kids home for the first time was a big deal and that people should know we were going out of town so they could keep an eye on the place for us."

"Good point," Robert muttered.

After that there wasn't much else to say, at least for the time being. Robert pressed down on the accelerator and the needle on the speedometer climbed to eighty.

If he kept this speed up, they would be able to make it home in less time than the remaining thirty-five minutes that the car's clock was indicating.

The moment he cracked a smile that Julia was actually letting him drive this fast without getting on him about being a "lunatic behind the wheel" was when he saw red and blue in his rearview.

"Shit me sideways!"

"What?"

"It's the fuzz!"

Robert eased his right foot off the gas pedal and not only saw the needle on the speedometer start to go down, but also their chances of making it home in time.

For some reason he started to feel like they hadn't been meant to spend a relaxing weekend in the city. While still trying to convince himself that *his* kids were going to be safe *when* they finally returned home.

CHAPTER 22

AFTER CRASHING TO the floor, Mariam must have blacked out for a few minutes, because when she woke up, she was naked and lying on top of her father's table saw. Her arms and legs were bent at odd angles, tied to the table's legs. She tried to move them, but they wouldn't budge. She was able to move her head. Now there was some night light filtering in through the garage windows. Looking down her body, past her bare breasts, stomach, and pubic mound, she saw how she had been situated. Her buttocks and legs were resting on top of the table. Her legs were spread apart. The table saw's blade was six or seven inches below her. The blade's jagged teeth stared at her like she was a prime piece of birchwood. The blade looked like it was salivating, though Mariam knew it was probably only the oil that her father had rubbed on it to keep it running smooth and looking new. She didn't even want to think about what the blade would feel like cutting her...

She shook her head to clear the macabre thought.

"Looks like I got me a prime cut of hog right here," grunted the man, somewhere in the still-dark garage. "Oh, yes. A *very* prime cut, if I do say so myself. Yummy in my tummy!"

"Sick bastard," Mariam mumbled.

"Huh. What was that, my little piggy?"

"I said, you are one sick *bastard*!"

"Hey, hey now. What did I tell you about your mouth? I mean, I like my ladies dirty and all, but not with such sewage spewing out of their hole."

"Fuck you!"

"Tsk, tsk, tsk..."

"Shut up!"

"Oh, come on now, it wouldn't be that bad."

"What wouldn't be *that* bad?" Mariam asked.

"When I cut you up and eat you like the little piggy that you are, of course."

Mariam didn't quite know what to say after hearing what the long-haired man planned to do with her. She hoped that Vince hadn't already met the same fate as she was about to, though she doubted it as she didn't see any blood when she had first entered the garage and turned the light on. Unless this freak and his buddy cut him up inside the house with a filet knife or something, Mariam thought. She gagged and spit on the floor. She could feel the bile rising up into her mouth and wanted to vomit. She figured that if she did vomit, at least the sick bastard wouldn't try and kiss her.

He might be one sick puppy, but no one wants to kiss somebody after they've just thrown up.

Mariam then thought that even if she did throw up it wouldn't guarantee the man wouldn't try messing around with her, so in the end it really wouldn't matter.

He sticks his tongue in my mouth and I'll bite the fuc—

Mariam's thoughts went to where in the garage that man was right now. She couldn't hear his breathing, so she figured that he must be at the front or very back of the garage by her father's workbench.

That's when Mariam heard a *clack* and a bright light from the fluorescent bulbs that her father had installed in the ceiling filled the room.

* * *

The person carrying the shovel that had clobbered Nick wasn't still outside to see the light come on inside through the garage door's windows. If he was, he would have been able to run inside and save Mariam from the long-haired man. But now he was inside the house, looking for the kids that were apparently in trouble. Even after calling the hotel where their parents were staying, the man still wasn't positive that something bad was happening. Those inclinations were confirmed, however, after he had seen a man carrying a large knife come running from the back of the house; a man he quickly took care of with one swing of his spade.

The first thing he noticed inside was the broken glass from the back door. Then there were the open beer bottles, all warm to the touch. Whoever was inside the house had been there long enough for their drinks to get warm. This could possibly mean that the kids were in more trouble than he previously thought.

Moving through the dining room, the person that he had seen fall on top of Mariam was still lying on the floor. His neck had been slashed and his head was lying at an odd angle in relation to his body. The blood was now coagulating, forming a nice oozy circle around the person's head and torso. There were red streak marks indicating the body had been moved at some point.

Moving past the body, the Shovel entered the living room and began to look around. The television and lights were off. It didn't look like there had been any sort of struggle in the room.

Shovel exited the living room, turned and walked down a narrow hallway.

Nearing the end of the hallway, he noticed something lying on the floor. At first it looked like a line of rope, but bending down and picking it up with his free hand, it turned out to be an extension cord. Following the cord, it ended in a knot on the partially open bathroom door. Dropping the cord, Shovel entered the bathroom. The window was open. A cool breeze was drifting into the room, fluttering the open curtain. There was some debris on the floor, but he didn't bother to inspect it. It didn't really matter what the items were, the kids weren't in the bathroom.

Exiting the bathroom and turning right, Shovel walked back down the hallway, turned left and started up the dark staircase. Shadows danced on the wallpaper from a light coming from the top of the stairs.

After a few slow minutes, Shovel came to the top of the stairs and noticed the light was coming from a partially open door on the right.

Slowly moving up to the door, he moved the shovel to his left shoulder and leaned an ear close to the door. There wasn't anyone talking or doing *anything* in the room, so he lowered the shovel to a "ready" position, put one foot in front of the other, and shoved the door the rest of the way open.

Shovel's eyes sprang open to the sight before them.

The boy screamed.

Shovel smiled.

CHAPTER 23

IT WAS HARD not to notice the man was naked. Not even his socks were still on. He had neatly folded his shirt, pants, and socks into a pile. They rested off to one side by his feet. His shoes were on top, weighing down the evil man's clothes so they wouldn't sprout wings and fly away.

Not only did the man have a mop of hair on top of his head, but the rest of his body was covered with it as well. His chest, arms, legs, and genital area looked like a forbidden black jungle. All that Mariam could see of the man's penis was the very tip, but she could tell that he was erect by how far it stuck away from his body. It looked wet and glistened in the faint moonlight coming into the garage. A twisted grin stretched across his narrow face. He licked his lips as he stared into Mariam's eyes. He didn't even blink when he started to speak.

"You're a beautiful young lady, you know that, don't you?"

"Uh, I don't know," Mariam muttered, wanting to cover up for nakedness.

"Sure you do. Hell, I just saw you the other day when me and my buddy were casing out the joint. You were out in the driveway washing a slick-looking Mercedes. You really soaped that sucker up. Man, just the way you were bent over the hood and moving that sponge around in circles made me wanna... And your hips, oh God, your hips...they seemed to move in sync with the movements of your arms while washing the car...of course, that music you were listening to on the jukebox probably helped, but still...you're a real piece of prime cut meat...but, you probably know that, don't you? Hell, sure you do. You wouldn't be parading that body of yours in that bikini in front of the house for any passersby to see if you didn't already know that."

"Uh, okay," is all Mariam could manage to get out.

"Anyway," continued the man, starting to inch his way closer to the table saw. Mariam watched him begin to walk closer to her. The head of his penis bounced with each step he took. "Seriously, though, you really are hot. I wonder if you feel as good as you look," the long-haired man said, licking his lips and moving closer still.

* * *

"I can't thank you enough for rescuing me, ya know?" Vince whispered as they started down the stairs.

"No problem," the man replied, hoisting the shovel onto one of his shoulders.

"Hey, before we start looking for Mariam, do you mind if I hit the bathroom?"

"All right, but try to make it a quick pit stop. We have no idea how long it's going to take us to find your sister."

"Okay. I'll try."

They continued down the stairs, turned right, and started down the hallway.

Up ahead, Vince could see the extension cord the two men had used to trap him and Mariam inside the bathroom. He cringed.

When he came to the door, he nodded to Shovel, stepped into the bathroom, and shut the door. He thought about thumbing down the lock button, but didn't. There was no need to now.

He was safe. He hoped Mariam was as well.

If not, he prayed they found her before the two men hurt her.

He sat down on the toilet.

His bowels exploded under him.

He felt better already.

* * *

Even after being issued a citation, 82 in a 65, Robert had quickly climbed up to his previous speed shortly after the officer let them drive away. He knew if he was able to keep the speed up, this time they'd be home in no more than twenty or so minutes.

He looked over at his wife and winked.

CHAPTER 24

"DON'T YOU DARE touch me, you filthy piece of trash," Mariam hissed as the long-haired man began to run his rough hands up her calves. He rubbed her kneecaps like you would a bald friend's head. A wide grin spread across the man's face.

"Hummm...mighty smooth legs you got here," the long-haired man said, licking his lips. Mariam noticed saliva dribbling out one of the corners of his mouth. Even though he had yet to touch any private areas, she still felt like she was being violated. He moved his hands up to Mariam's thighs.

"God, you are so beautiful. 'Tis a shame I'm gonna have to kill such a sweet young thing as yourself."

"But...but why? You don't have to kill me, mister. Hey, listen. I swear, if you just take what you want out of the house and leave me and my brother alone, I won't tell anybody about what happened here. Okay?"

The man laughed.

"You really think I'm gonna believe that, huh? Here is what's going to happen, okay. I'm gonna have a little fun with you, and then your brother, and then me and my friend Nick are going to steal all your parents' shit. Now, how does *that* sound?"

"Sounds like *shit*," Mariam hissed.

The man laughed again and then said, "Well, I don't think you're in any position to make any requests or demands now, are ya?"

"Uhhh...I guess not. But..."

"Hey! There will be no b—b—buts around here, missy. The only but is going to be your *butt*, or should I say ass. And damn, what a mighty fine ass it is. I had the pleasure of kneading it like a bowl of fresh bread dough after I stripped ya, but before tying you down to this fine machine, of course."

She screamed.

* * *

"Pardon my French, but what the hell was that?" Vince whispered as he and Shovel exited the back door of the house.

They stopped and listened for another scream, but one didn't come.

"I hate to tell ya this, Vince. But I think that was your sister. At least we know she's close by though. Come on," Shovel said, waving for Vince to follow him into the back yard.

"But, where in the hell could she be? Hey, I bet she's in—"

Another scream ripped through the air.

Then another sound came resonating through the damp air. But this one didn't sound like any kind of scream. It was more of a whine.

"What is *that*, now?" Vince whispered.

"I'm not totally sure. But hey, let me ask you a question. Is it just me or did that sound like it was coming from the garage?"

"Yeah, could be. Why?"

"Ah, well...I hate to ask you this, Vince...but doesn't your father have his wood-working equipment in there?"

Vince's stomach dropped. He felt like he needed to run back into the house and plop down onto the toilet again. He clenched his buttocks so nothing would come out. He knew now wasn't the time for another bowel movement. That, and he needed to be brave for Mariam's sake. He followed Shovel along the side of the house. When Shovel came to the corner, next to the garage, he abruptly stopped. Vince nearly ran into his back.

"Hey, what's the big idea—"

"Shhh! I've gotta check on somebody before we go any further."

"Check on *somebody*? Who?"

"I'm assuming it's one of the guys that broke into your house. After calling your parents, I grabbed this here shovel, I came across the street and started to have a look around. I looked in your front windows but didn't see much. That is when I decided to have a closer look and came around the back of the house to see if they could have come in there, ya know. That's when I ran into this *somebody* coming around the corner."

"Wait. You called my parents? And so why do you have to *check* on him? What, is he hiding over there or something?"

"First. Yes, I called your parents. Hopefully they got my message and are on their way. Second. The guy isn't *hiding* over here; he's more like lying on the ground with a bashed-in face. Well, at least I hope he still is."

"Bashed-in face?"

The Shovel patted the spade and smiled back at Vince.

"Ah, gotcha. You laid his ass out, eh?"

"Hey, watch your language. Ya know, I am still an adult."

"Sorry about that. But seriously, good going on that."

Shovel smiled again, then turned away to look around the corner of the house.

His mouth fell open. He could hear Vince asking, "Well?" behind him. He wanted to turn around and tell him yes, the guy was still unconscious and on the ground, but he couldn't.

The man was gone.

And so was the large butcher knife he'd been carrying before Shovel put the hurt on him.

Shovel took a deep breath and turned around just in time to see a dark shadow coming up behind Vince. His knife was the only thing about the man that Shovel could make out.

Shovel wanted to scream out to warn Vince of the oncoming man, but couldn't. He felt the words stuck in his mouth, and bile rising up his throat.

"Well?" Vince asked again.

Then the man's knife plunged deep into his back and he let out a bloodcurdling scream.

* * *

"How much longer do you think we have?" Julia asked again.

Robert looked down at the green numbers on the dash and then said, "As long as traffic stays thinned out like this, I'd say no more than ten, fifteen minutes."

"Okay."

Robert looked over at his wife and watched her continue to bite her now-bleeding nails.

He cringed and then pressed down on the accelerator.

CHAPTER 25

THE LONG-HAIRED MAN pulled away from Mariam and turned to look toward the garage door. He muttered, "Yum, sounds like more meat," but had an annoyed look on his face. John knew he had to see what the commotion was about, and figured that Nick had the upper hand with whatever was going on outside the garage. Since he had started to touch Mariam, he had slowly inched his naked body on top of the table saw to get a better angle of her trembling body. Now he was climbing off. *Thank God*, Mariam said to herself, as the man now stood on the floor next to the table. He was more turned on now than before he had started messing around with the girl. He bent down to retrieve the closed straight razor, but instead of using it on the laid-out flesh before him, Mariam watched as he strode toward the door. She blew out a sigh of relief. Then she heard him say, "Wait a minute," and he turned back around to face her.

"Well, hell. I almost forgot to switch on that there saw."

"*What?*" burst out of Mariam.

"That there saw you're lying on. I almost forgot to turn it on to make sure the events that have taken place remain between you and I...well, at least me and your ghost, that is."

"Uhhh...seriously, sir...I promise I won't tell anybody about you breaking into the house, killing the doctor, or messing around with me, really. In fact, if you want the honest to God truth...I was sorta enjoying what you were doing," Mariam lied.

"Really?"

"Well, sure. It's not every day I get to be tied down like the bad girl that I am and have some strapping older guy mess around with me. It's sorta fun," Mariam said, and then winked. She had never been the best liar, but hoped this time she would be able to get away with it. Of course she didn't like what the man had been doing to her, but at this point, she didn't see any other option. This might be her only way out of the situation, so she was going to play the role of the naughty undersexed teenage girl for all that it was worth. She licked her lips and winked again.

"Hummm…sure would be nice to actually be able to have a piece of that fine body of yours. Shit. I bet you would enjoy it, too. But…"

Mariam knew she wasn't going to like the "but" that was coming.

"But, *honestly*, as you put it…I just can't trust you. I was taught tell by my mentor to never leave someone alive that sees your face when you're doing a job…and even though I would love to have you around a little while longer…I just can't risk it."

The long-haired man walked back over to the table, still carrying the straight razor in one hand, and flipped the "On" switch with the other.

A high-pitched whining sound filled the room. Mariam could feel the slight breeze from the spinning blade against her thighs.

The man then walked behind Mariam. She had to tilt her head way back to see him. He was now staring down at her. He still had the closed straight razor in one hand, but now in the other he had a length of rope.

He gave the rope a pull. Mariam started moving downward.

She hadn't noticed it before, but she hadn't been lying directly on top of the table saw. Yes, technically she was on top of the table, but she was lying on a piece of plywood. There was no way she could have noticed before, but the long-haired man had cut a hole in the wood right above her head, fed a length of rope through it, and tied the end off to an eye-hook on the far wall where her father kept his small hand tools. The other thing that Mariam didn't notice, and couldn't have even if she wanted to, was that attached to the bottom of the piece of plywood were casters.

That was why she was moving downward.

Toward the blades.

She didn't even have time to scream before the man leaned down, kissed her on top of the forehead, and walked away.

When the lights went out again, Mariam tried to let out a scream for help.

But she knew no one would hear it over the loud whining of the table saw's blades.

That she was slowly rolling toward.

CHAPTER 26

VINCE'S BELLY ITCHED as the sticky grass rubbed against him. The man was sprawled on his back, making it impossible for him to push himself off the ground. As bad as the grass and the bloody faced man's body felt on top of him, it was small peanuts in comparison to the knife that was still lodged in his back. The man wiggled the blade around in circles. Vince screamed again. He tried to lift his face off the ground to look for the man that had rescued him from being tied down to his bed, but the bloody faced man pushed his head down with his other hand before he had the chance to have a good look around.

He screamed again. The uncut grass in the back yard swept into his mouth when he inhaled to let out the next violent scream. He coughed and pushed the blades out with his tongue. He felt the man's penis push against his buttocks and felt his stomach turn sour. He was still too young to know *everything* about sex, but had seen enough on television to know what equipment was used during the act.

Then the heavy weight of the man was gone. He felt like his skin was on fire as the knife was ripped from his back. The strange part was, it hadn't felt like he had *climbed* off him. He had been enjoying twisting the knife in his back and dry humping his clothed buttocks too much. No, but he had *somehow* gotten off him.

He flipped over in time to see the man flying backwards through the air. He was still holding the knife in his hand.

He landed a few feet away.

Shovel ran over, lifted the spade high into the air and brought it straight down. As the blade pierced the man's neck, there was a crack and a wet *thunk*. Then Shovel brought back one of his boots and kicked the man's face. There was a *thud*, like a cantaloupe being stomped on, and the head went flying through the air into the dark back yard.

As Shovel was walking back over to Vince, he was smiling.

"Nice going," Vince huffed, pushing himself off the ground. His back felt like he had been stuck with a hot poker. "My back feels like…"

Something *whished* by the side of his head.

Figuring it was just an annoying insect, he turned his head around to make sure a swarm of them wasn't following the sweet smell of the oozing blood on his back.

It was just in time to see a long-haired man running toward them.

He turned back around to see if Shovel noticed who was coming at them, but only saw Shovel falling to the ground.

A long straight razor was embedded in the front of his neck.

CHAPTER 27

SHE DIDN'T WANT to look, but had to. A *zzzeee* sound filled the dark garage as the table saw's sharp blade met the plywood that Mariam was lying on. It would only be a matter of a minute or so, with the speed she was rolling, until the blades met her flesh. She knew then it would be bye-bye, Mariam, hello, Heaven. She hoped it would be Heaven, anyway. She figured it would be. She hadn't been the best daughter or teenager in the world, but God is forgiving, so she figured she'd be all right. Maybe I'll spend a few years in Purgatory, but then I should be good to go, Mariam thought.

She raised her head and saw how easily the blade was cutting through the wood. Splinters and sawdust were flying this way and that. Some landed on her legs. She wanted to kick her legs, to get the reminder of impending doom off of her, but she couldn't move them that much. She tried wiggling her buttocks on the plywood she was lying on, but each time she did, she felt like a hundred splinters were chewing at her bare skin. Mariam knew she only had a limited amount of time before the blades started digging themselves into the soft flesh in between her legs, so she rested her head back onto the wood and cited the Lord's Prayer to herself.

She hoped that the Big Man above would have pity on her soul and let her keep it a little while longer.

How that was going to be possible, she had no idea.

CHAPTER 28

MARIAM WAS SURROUNDED by light. The fear and anger at what had been happening to her was suddenly gone. She felt at peace. A soothing sound, almost like a harp playing beautiful music, was all around her. She felt like she was floating through the air. All sense of gravity was gone. She felt full of love, understanding, and forgiveness toward what the long-haired man had done to her and her brother. How she missed Vince and hoped that they would be reunited at any moment here in Heaven. She was sure of it. *If I made it here, surely a sweet nine-year-old did as well.*

The music stopped.

Mariam opened her eyes and found Vince staring down at her.

He was sheathed in blood.

What the hell...

"Mariam...Mariam, are you okay?" Vince said, slapping her sister's cheeks.

"Huh...wha..."

"I said, are you *okay?*"

"Uh, yeah, I guess so. What the hell happened here?"

"All hell broke loose, that's what."

"Bu...but, what about that crazy dude with the long hair...he'll kill you if he sees you in here trying to..."

"*Shhh*...hush, hush, now. There's no need to be afraid anymore, Mariam... Everything has been taken care of."

Vince then untied his sister, helped her into her clothes, and led her from the well-lit garage back into the dark back yard.

CHAPTER 29

WHEN THEY REACHED the back yard, Mariam's mouth fell open. She couldn't believe the carnage that lay in front of her.

In the middle of the yard, she saw a tall man, with a shovel lying on the ground beside him. His throat had a deep bloody gash in it. Leaning down, she was able to get a better view and realized who it was: Mr. Henderson, from across the street. Vince began to tell her how he had come to his rescue, untying him from the bed, and how he had decapitated one of the burglars. She didn't exactly know why, but Mariam started to cry after Vince finished the story of how he had helped him. Now she felt bad about always assuming he had been some chauvinistic asshole, always trying to check out her body when she was out washing the car or sunning herself clad in her bikini.

She continued to follow her brother until they reached the two other men.

The long-haired one was lying on top of the burglar who had lost his head. Vince reminded her that Mr. Henderson had done that to him. Mariam started to cry, again, at the memory of a good man that had been killed in such an awful way.

Vince then told her how the events had unfolded and who had died when and in what way. Though, he didn't go into much detail about how the long-haired man had met his demise. Mariam had a pretty good idea. Without even seeing the front of long hair, Mariam was able to see several long, deep gashes across the man's back, buttocks, and chest. Mariam also noticed a shriveled-up piece of flesh that looked like a tube sticking out of the man's mouth, but decided not to ask Vince how it had gotten there. Since the men were definitely both dead—the one had lost his head and the other had been badly sliced and diced—Mariam didn't feel the need to see the front of long hair's body. She had seen enough of it already, and just knowing that he would never hurt another person was satisfaction enough. She did want *one* item from the ordeal—the long-haired man's razor—since he had not only tried to use it on her, but it had been used to kill her neighbor and, in the end, the sick bastard himself. She didn't see it anywhere.

She turned to Vince, who was surprisingly calm and collected.

"Hey, did you by chance happen to keep the—"

Brightness suddenly filled the strip of yard between the house and the garage.

Mariam knew without even running over and checking who it was.

Her parents.

She knew she had a world of explaining to them what had happened.

But she, Vince, and the house were safe.

And since that had been their only stipulation for the weekend, if they raised a bitchfest about the rest, well then, that was just going to be tough shit and they would just have to deal with it.

Mariam turned and put her arm around Vince's shoulder, and they walked *together* toward the light.

ABOUT THE AUTHOR

TY SCHWAMBERGER is an award-winning author & editor in the horror genre. He is the author of a novel, multiple novellas, collections and editor on several anthologies. In addition, he's had many short stories published online and in print. Three stories, "Cake Batter" (released in 2010), "House Call" (first released in June 2013) and "The Halloween Hero" (optioned in 2014), have been optioned for film adaptation. He is an Active Member of the International Thriller Writers. Learn more at http://tyschwamberger.com.

HOUSE CALL

SCREENPLAY BY SHANNON CASTO

SCENE 1
SETTING: INTERIOR HOUSE, VINCE'S BEDROOM
CHARACTERS: VINCE AND MARIAM

FADE IN:

Mariam, a 16-year-old girl, pulls a thermometer from the lips of her sleeping nine-year-old brother, Vince, and looks at it. It reads 103 degrees. Mariam looks distressed and sets the thermometer on the nightstand next to a glass of water, some Pepto, and some children's aspirin. Leaving the door open a crack, Mariam leaves her brother's room and starts for the staircase.

SCENE 2
SETTING: HOUSE INTERIOR, KITCHEN
CHARACTERS: MARIAM, VOICES OF DR. AND MRS. BLYTHWORTH

The house is dark. Mariam enters the kitchen and starts across the tile floor to the refrigerator and picks up a note that says: Paradise Hotel – 555-8861. She walks over to a phone hanging on the wall by the back door. She picks it up and starts punching in the numbers. On the third ring, someone picks up.

HOTEL EMPLOYEE
Thank you for calling Paradise Hotel, my name is Gene, how may I help you?

Mariam hangs up.

MARIAM
(Muttering to herself) It's late, and they are probably asleep. Either that or busy doing *something* I don't want to think about.

Mariam picks the phone back up from its base on the wall and punches in a new set of numbers and waits. It rings five or six times. Mariam is about ready to hang up when a groggy sounding woman's voice comes across the receiver.

MRS. BLYTHWORTH

Hel...hello...

MARIAM

Uh, yes, Mrs. Blythworth, this is Mariam Oster. My family and I are patients of your husband's.

Mariam hears the sleepy woman give a deep huff and then the line is quiet for a few seconds. The next voice that comes across the phone is the deep voice of Dr. Blythworth.

DR. BLYTHWORTH

Hello. This is Dr. Blythworth. Who did you say you were again?

MARIAM

Oh, hi, Dr. Blythworth. This is Mariam Oster. I'm Robert and Julia's daughter.

DR. BLYTHWORTH

Oh, yes. What can I do for you, Mariam?

MARIAM

Well, you know my brother, Vince? He is a patient of yours as well and ummm...he's not feeling very well and...

DR. BLYTHWORTH

(Cutting in) Mariam, it is late. Why don't you have your parents call my office in the morning and schedule an appointment and I'll see your brother at that time. But, if it is an emergency, I suggest you tell your parents to take Vince to the ER. I can follow up with the hospital in the morning for your brother's status.

MARIAM

Well...that is sorta the problem, Dr. Blythworth.

DR. BLYTHWORTH

What is?

MARIAM

My parents. See, they're out of town for the weekend and left me in charge. They really don't want to be bothered. Plus I told them if anything did come up I would handle it myself.

DR. BLYTHWORTH

I see.

MARIAM

And, well…Vince just came down with something tonight. It was after dinner and he started complaining about his stomach not feeling very well. I told him to take some pink stuff and go lay down. He seemed to be doing fine until a few hours ago. But that is when the fever came. It has gone up each hour ever since. So, you see, Dr. Blythworth…I really can't call my parents. They'll never let me stay home alone with Vince again if I don't take care of this myself.

DR. BLYTHWORTH

I see. Well, why don't you just take your brother to the ER by yourself? If I remember correctly, you're sixteen now, correct?

MARIAM

Yes, Doctor…I *am* sixteen. But I only have my permit right now. Mom and Dad are taking me next week to take my driving test. Plus, even if I did have my license, Mom and Dad took the only car, so I couldn't take Vince to the ER even if I wanted to.

Dr. Blythworth doesn't reply right away. Mariam can hear him and his wife talking in the background. A moment later there is a ruffling sound like he is taking his hand away from the phone and his voice returns.

DR. BLYTHWORTH

Okay, Mariam. I tell you what. I don't make house calls, not for years now, but because of your situation I'll make an exception this time. What's your address?

MARIAM

It's 1709 Manning Street, and thank…

DR. BLYTHWORTH

Okay, got it. See you in thirty minutes.

He hangs up.

MARIAM

(Hanging up the phone) What a jerk.

She walks over to the fridge and draws a pitcher of lemonade out, takes a tall glass from the cupboard, fills it and puts the pitcher back into the fridge. She sets the glass on the counter, opens up the freezer and pulls out a red Popsicle, then closes the freezer, grabs her glass of lemonade and the Popsicle and starts back up the stairs to Vince's room.

SCENE 3
SETTING: HOUSE INTERIOR, VINCE'S ROOM
CHARACTERS: MARIAM AND VINCE

Taking a sip from her lemonade, Mariam pushes Vince's door open and walks into the room. A small night-light is on beside the bed. It casts an eerie glow over the small lump in the bed. Mariam walks up to the bed, puts her glass on the nightstand and leans over her nine-year-old brother.

MARIAM

Vince…you awake…I thought you might like a Popsicle. (gently shaking Vince)

VINCE

Huh. Wha…

MARIAM

It's me, Mariam. Sorry to wake you, but I thought it would be a good idea to check your temperature again.

VINCE

Oh, okay.

Vince pushes himself up and leans against the headboard. Mariam takes the thermometer off the nightstand, wipes its metal tip off with a Kleenex and puts it under Vince's tongue. A minute later the thermometer gives off a beep. Mariam pulls it from Vince's mouth and looks it at. It reads 103.5 degrees. Mariam looks upset.

VINCE

(Pulling the covers up to his sweaty neck) Well, what is it? 'Cause I think I'm feeling a little better now.

MARIAM

(Pushing a button on the thermometer to turn it off) Well, it looks like it's going up. So you better have this. (handing the Popsicle to Vince)

VINCE

Wow, thanks. Red, my favorite.

Mariam picks up her lemonade from the nightstand and takes another drink.

MARIAM

Well, I've got some good news. (setting her glass back down onto the nightstand)

VINCE

Mom and Dad are coming home?

MARIAM

No. Not that. I called Dr. Blythworth, and he said he's coming over to take a look at you.

VINCE

Oh. Don't you think it's a better idea to have Mom and Dad come home?

MARIAM

Nah. This'll be fine. Besides, I told Mom and Dad that I could handle a weekend taking care of you and the house while they have a relaxing weekend alone together.

VINCE

Still. I think you should call Mom and Dad and at least let them know what is going on. (He takes another lick from the melting Popsicle)

MARIAM

Nah. This'll be fine. The doctor will come over, take a look at you and probably give you some sort of medicine to feel better. Then we don't have to call Mom and Dad and wake them up at this hour. By the time they get home on Sunday, you'll be feeling better and no one will be the wiser.

VINCE

Yeah, I guess that will work. But what if Dr. Blythworth mentions something to Mom or Dad at one of their next appointments? Then how are you going to explain to them that I had a bad fever and didn't call them?

Mariam shrugs her shoulders, picks up her lemonade and starts toward the bedroom door.

VINCE

Hey, where are you going?

MARIAM

Downstairs. I won't be able to hear Dr. Blythworth at the door when he gets here if I am sitting up here in your room. Don't worry though. He said he wouldn't be long. But, if he is taking a while to get here, I'll come back up and check on you in a little while. Okay?

VINCE

(Sucking on the remainder of his Popsicle) Okay.

Mariam exits the room.

SCENE 4A
SETTING: HOUSE INTERIOR, LIVING ROOM
CHARACTERS: MARIAM

Mariam makes her way to the living room. It is dark, except for a low-wattage lamp sitting on a small table at the far end of the room. She plops down on the couch. Her eyes are heavy. She gently slaps her face a few times and then picks up the remote and turns on the television. She starts to flip through the channels. Her eyes get heavy again. She tries a few times keeping herself awake by forcing her eyes open really wide, but her eyes close all the way and she drifts off. She hears a scream and jumps up and starts running up the stairs.

SCENE 5
SETTING: HOUSE INTERIOR, VINCE'S ROOM
CHARACTERS: MARIAM AND VINCE

Mariam bursts into her brother's room, and she sees the familiar lump under the covers. She lets out a little sigh and walks toward the bed. As she gets to the edge of the bed, she feels something wet on the floor. She looks down and sees she has stepped in a dark puddle of something. She suddenly looks uneasy and slowly reaches out and pulls the covers back. Vince lies there dead, gutted. Mariam screams and collapses onto the floor.

SCENE 4B
SETTING: HOUSE INTERIOR, LIVING ROOM
CHARACTERS: MARIAM

Mariam jolts awake on the couch drenched in sweat, relieved *it is only a nightmare*. She stands up, stretches her arms over her head and looks at the clock on the mantel above the fireplace. It reads *12:17*. She looks toward the stairs and walks over and heads up.

SCENE 6
SETTING: HOUSE INTERIOR, VINCE'S ROOM
CHARACTERS: MARIAM

Mariam walks into Vince's bedroom. The bed is empty. She looks relieved and then instantly worried. She reaches over and flicks on the light. She turns out of the room and starts back down the stairs.

SCENE 7
SETTING: HOUSE INTERIOR, HALLWAY OUTSIDE BATHROOM
CHARACTERS: MARIAM, VOICE OF VINCE

Mariam walks down the hallway. As she nears the end of the hallway, there is a crack of light coming from under the bathroom door. She goes up to the bathroom door and knocks.

MARIAM
Vince? Vince…you in there? You okay?

Mariam hears a rustling sound on the other side of the door but no response. She knocks again. No response.

MARIAM
Hey, Vince. It's me. I'm going to come in, okay?

Just as she is twisting the knob on the bathroom door, she hears another rustling sound just before she hears Vince's voice.

VINCE
No, wait. Don't come in! I'm using the restroom right now.

MARIAM
Oh. Oh, okay. Well, take your time and let me know if you need anything, sweetie. I'll be in the kitchen.

VINCE
Okay, thanks.

SCENE 8A
SETTING: HOUSE INTERIOR, KITCHEN AND ENTRY
CHARACTERS: MARIAM

Mariam heads into the kitchen and sits at the counter. She looks first at the clock that now reads *12:22* and then looks at the phone on the wall and gets up and goes to it.

MARIAM

(Mumbling) This is getting ridiculous.

She picks up the receiver and punches in the doctor's number and waits. Five…six…seven rings go off in her ear. No one picks up the other end of the line.

MARIAM

(Setting the receiver down, hard) Damn.

She walks to the front entrance way and looks out the window next to the door. The street directly in front of her house is dark and wet from the rain. She notices there are lights on across the street at the Henderson house.

SCENE 9A MARIAM FLASHBACK
SETTING: HOUSE INTERIOR, MARIAM'S BEDROOM
CHARACTERS: MARIAM

Mariam is 15 and puts on her yellow and blue polka-dotted bikini, then trots downstairs.

SCENE 9B MARIAM FLASHBACK
SETTING: HOUSE INTERIOR, KITCHEN, GARAGE, EXTERIOR, DRIVEWAY
CHARACTERS: MARIAM AND MR. HENDERSON

Mariam grabs a bottled water out of the fridge and heads out to the garage and gathers a bucket, sponge, car soap, a chamois, and a few rags. She walks out the open garage door to the side of the house, turns on the water and drags the hose to the front. She sprays the car and starts to wash it, constantly peering over her shoulder, hoping someone would drive by. No one does. But then she feels like someone is watching her. One of the times she is bent over in front of the car with her back to the street, she turns her head and sees her neighbor, Mr. Henderson, coming across the street toward her. He is carrying a can of soda in one hand, a beer in the other, and has a goofy grin on his face. Mariam quickly stands up when she sees him crossing the street toward her and moves her hands and arms in front of herself awkwardly trying to find a way to conceal herself. Mr. Henderson finishes crossing the street and stops a few feet in front of her.

MR. HENDERSON

Hey there, Mariam. How's it going?

MARIAM

Ah, not too bad, Mr. Henderson. Nice day, eh?

MR. HENDERSON

Yeah, but sure is a hot one. Thought you could use a drink. (holding out the can of soda for Mariam to take)

MARIAM

Oh, no thanks, Mr. Henderson. I've got a water over there by the garage door. But thanks anyway.

MR. HENDERSON

Oh, come on. Take it. It's nice and cold. Heck, you've been out here for a while now.

Mariam looks uneasy at the idea that he had been watching her.

MR. HENDERSON

…So that drink of yours is probably warm by now.

Mariam takes the drink from him.

MR. HENDERSON

So, anyway...how's your summer going?

MARIAM

Hey, thanks for the drink, Mr. Henderson. I've really got to finish scrubbing and rinse this sucker before the suds dry and leave water marks on the car.

Mr. Henderson smiles and backs up a few feet to the sidewalk and stops. Mariam is uneasy but goes back to washing the car even with Mr. Henderson blatantly staring at her.

SCENE 8B
SETTING: HOUSE INTERIOR, ENTRY
CHARACTERS: MARIAM

MARIAM

(Muttering as she stands at the window and continues to watch for Dr. Blythworth) Damn, if he could only see me now. (Pause) Ugh! What the hell am I thinking? "If he could only see me now." What the hell is that all about?

Mariam backs away from the window and checks to see if Vince is still in the bathroom, but the door is open and the light is out. She walks into the kitchen.

SCENE 10
SETTING: HOUSE INTERIOR, KITCHEN AND ENTRY
CHARACTERS: MARIAM AND DR. BLYTHWORTH

In the kitchen, Mariam makes her way over to the phone. She picks it up and starts to dial the doctor's home number. Right when a connection is made and she thinks she hears the doctor's wife on the other end, the doorbell rings. She slams the phone down on its cradle and rushes to the front door. She grabs the doorknob and is about to unlock the deadbolt with her other hand when she decides to first check *who* is at the door. She puts her eye up to the peephole and sees another eye staring back at her. She screams.

Arms flying and legs staggering backwards, Mariam is still screaming when her butt hits the floor. She takes a deep breath and lets it out. Assuming it is just Dr. Blythworth at the front door, she picks herself up, unlocks the inner door, and swings it open.

It is Dr. Blythworth. He has thinning brown hair with silver specks, a brown wool jacket and grey slacks. He is clutching a black bag in his right hand, and he is leaning against the screen door in such a way that if he puts any more of his weight onto it, he will rip the screen and crash right through. Mariam steps up to the door and takes a good look at the top of Dr. Blythworth's head.

MARIAM

Dr. Blythworth? You okay?

She taps a finger on the doctor's head through the screen. He does not respond.

MARIAM

Doctor...

The physician's body falls away from the screen and slumps to the porch floor. His head connects with the porch with a thump.

MARIAM

Oh, my god...doctor...

Mariam tries to push open the screen door, but his feet are in the way. She can only push the door open a few inches.

MARIAM

Doctor, please...

Mariam puts her weight against the door and pushes. The doctor's legs begin to bend, letting the screen door open enough for Mariam to squeeze out of the house. She peers down at the doctor. He isn't moving. Without getting closer or a light, Mariam can't tell if he is breathing or not. She pulls open the screen door, reaches around the door jamb and flicks the porch light on. She screams again as she sees blood flow out of a deep gash in the doctor's neck. The blood runs off the porch and down the front steps.

SCENE 11A
SETTING: HOUSE EXTERIOR, CAR INTERIOR
CHARACTERS: JOHN, NICK, MARIAM AND DR. BLYTHWORTH

Thugs John and Nick sit outside in their car, and watch Mariam react to the dead doctor.

NICK

I still don't know about this, man.

John is in the driver's seat laughing at the sight. He turns to his friend.

JOHN

Huh? What did you say?

NICK

I said... I don't know about this, man. I mean...it's one thing to break into people's houses and steal their shit, but this is going a little far, don't you think?

JOHN

You worry too much, man.

John takes the last hit on his cigarette and flicks the butt into the street.

JOHN

Besides, I told you there is some prime shit in that house. It'll bring us some major coinage, so why you bitchin'?

NICK

'Cause, man. I didn't sign up to be part of no murder. Shit. You murdered that dude in cold blood.

JOHN

Hey, you want part of the take or not, man?

NICK

Never said I didn't.

JOHN

Shit. You might as well have. You're over there complaining about *me* cutting some asshole's throat you don't even know.

NICK

Doesn't matter if I know him or not. You still didn't have to kill him.

JOHN

Sure as shit did. 'Cause we saw the parents leaving with a suitcase so we know they're gonna be gone for at least tonight and maybe the whole weekend. We can not only rob the place, but have a little fun at the same time. Besides, do you really think if we broke in there, that he wouldn't have put up a fight?

NICK

Well…yeah…I mean…I'm sure he would have…but still…we could have tied him up or something.

JOHN

Yeah, well…whatever, man.

John pulls another cigarette from his pack and lights it with the car lighter. He takes in a deep pull and blows the smoke out his nose. He watches the girl across the street try to figure out what to do next and the scene fades.

SCENE 12A JOHN FLASHBACK
SETTING: HOUSE EXTERIOR AND INTERIOR
CHARACTERS: JOHN AND ROCK

John and his mentor, Rock, quietly work the back door of a dark house open with a crowbar and enter. They instantly hear screaming coming from the upstairs of the house. They creep upstairs.

SCENE 12B JOHN FLASHBACK
SETTING: HOUSE INTERIOR, BEDROOM
CHARACTERS: JOHN AND ROCK, MAN AND WOMAN

John and Rock enter a bedroom to find a man and woman locked in some sort of twisted sexual position, the woman screaming with delight as they go at it. Rock enters the bedroom first with a hard kick, sending the door flying open. He charges into the room, runs to the bed, slices the man's neck with a straight razor and throws him off his wife, who is now choking from all the blood that is raining down on her from the deep gash in her husband's neck. She starts screaming and thrashing on the bed. Rock reaches down, pulls the woman by her hair closer to him, and slices her throat from ear to ear.

SCENE 12C JOHN FLASHBACK
SETTING: HOUSE INTERIOR AND EXTERIOR
CHARACTERS: JOHN AND ROCK AND POLICE

John and Rock rob the house, taking anything small and valuable. As they exit the house and start down the driveway to the getaway car parked across the street, two marked patrol cars screech to a stop in front of the house and cops come jumping out with their guns drawn. They tell Rock and John to freeze. John does. Rock doesn't. As Rock continues down the driveway, he calls over his shoulder to John.

ROCK

Get outta here, man. Save yourself. They'll never take me alive. I'm never going back.

John turns and runs. Rock is carrying his bag of loot in one hand and his open straight razor in the other.

ROCK

Come on, pigs! Show me what you got!

John looks over his shoulder once and sees Rock go down in a hail of gunfire. He runs through the back yard of the couple's house, into the alley, and then hightails it out of the area. As he runs down the alley, he keeps hold of the bag that is carrying his part of the take from the house.

SCENE 11B
SETTING: HOUSE EXTERIOR, CAR INTERIOR
CHARACTERS: JOHN, NICK, MARIAM AND DR. BLYTHWORTH

Still staring at the house, John notices Mariam turn and run back into the house. He smiles and looks at Nick.

JOHN

Jam the cell phones. It's time.

Nick takes a small black device from the glove box and hits a button.

SCENE 13
SETTING: HOUSE INTERIOR, VINCE'S BEDROOM AND MARIAM'S BEDROOM
CHARACTERS: MARIAM AND VINCE

Mariam runs inside and races to the top of the stairs, rounds the corner and races into her room. She grabs her cell phone off the bed and turns it on. There is no signal.

MARIAM

Shit, shit, shit!

She throws it back on the bed and runs into Vince's room. Vince is still in bed, asleep. Mariam rushes over and shakes his shoulder.

MARIAM

Vince…wake up…something happened to Dr. Blythworth.

VINCE

(Beginning to stir, opens his eyes and looks up) Wha…what's going on?

MARIAM

The doctor… Dr. Blythworth… he's *hurt* bad… maybe even dead… we've got to get outta here!

VINCE

(Trying to process) What are you talking about, Mariam?

MARIAM

Remember…how I told you that Dr. Blythworth was coming over to take a look at you…

VINCE

Yeah…so?

MARIAM

Well, he's here alright…but…but, somebody attacked him before I could get to the door…he's dead, Vince.

VINCE

DEAD!

MARIAM

Yes. Now get your butt in gear. Put on some clothes and come with me.

Vince scrambles out of bed trying to find something to put on.

VINCE

Where...where's my Care Bears shirt?

Mariam is peaking outside the door making sure no one is coming up the stairs.

MARIAM

I don't know, Vince. It doesn't matter what you put on. Just find something to cover yourself with.

A moment later Vince is done getting dressed, including socks and tennis shoes. Mariam motions for Vince to follow her, and they race down the hall to Mariam's bedroom. Mariam is wearing only a tank top and cotton shorts. She selects a pair of running socks, puts them on, then runs over to the closet to get her running shoes. She finds them and sits down on the floor to put them on. She glances up at Vince and sees the look of fear on his face. Mariam quickly laces up her shoes, stands up and goes to the bedroom door.

She slowly peeks around the door jamb and scans the dark hallway for movement. There is none. She grabs her brother by the hand and pulls him into the dark hallway. They hear the breaking of glass downstairs.

SCENE 14
SETTING: HOUSE INTERIOR, KITCHEN AND DINING ROOM
CHARACTERS: JOHN AND NICK

Nick reaches through the broken pane of the back door to unlock it and he and John step into the house. They are in the kitchen. The room is dark except for a small light on above the stove.

JOHN

Come on, man. Start looking around.

NICK

In the kitchen?

JOHN

Hell yeah! You never know what sort of treasures people hide in strange places.

Nick nods and starts to search the drawer that is closest to him. John goes over to the fridge and pulls it open. A blast of light engulfs the room, startling Nick. John pulls two bottles of beer from the fridge, closes the door, and turns back to his friend, who is rummaging through the silverware drawer. John walks over and puts the cold bottle of beer on the back of Nick's neck. Nick jumps again.

NICK

Hey, man…what the hell?

JOHN

Oh, stop. It's just a beer, man. Enjoy.

Nick takes the bottle from John, twists off the top and takes a few gulps.

JOHN

Any luck over there? (He takes another drink of beer)

NICK

Nah. Nothing here. How about you?

JOHN

Nada.

They walk out of the kitchen and into the dining room. They notice a hutch in the far corner. They walk over, pull open the twin doors and look inside. John reaches into his pocket and pulls out a pen light and shines it in on the contents.

JOHN

Oh, yeah…this is some good shit right here. (motioning to Nick to open the canvas bag they had brought in with them)

NICK

NICK

Yeah, nice.

John proceeds to load the bag with the silver, then he waves his hand and they proceed out of the dining room. They come to the entrance way leading into the house. As they stand there with the moon, street, and porch lights flooding into the house, they see the dead guy still lying on the porch.

JOHN

Hey, Nick.

NICK

Yeah?

JOHN

We need to get this fucker off the porch.

NICK

Yeah, I was just thinking the same thing. But first things first. We need to kill that porch light.

JOHN

Good thinking.

John moves over to the front door and thumbs down the light switch. The porch goes mostly dark. Nick puts down his bag of goodies and follows John onto the front porch.

JOHN

You get his head and I'll get his feet.

NICK

Right.

Nick reaches under the guy's bloody head and grasps underneath his

114

arms. John grabs the guy's ankles.

                    JOHN
Okay, on the count of three. One...two...

They are only able to lift him an inch or so off the porch, but it is enough
for them to shuffle him into the house. John throws the guy's legs down
and closes the door. He dead bolts it.

                    JOHN
Damn, that guy is a heavy son of a bitch.

SCENE 15
SETTING: HOUSE INTERIOR, TOP OF THE STAIRS
CHARACTERS: MARIAM AND VINCE

Standing at the top of the stairs, Mariam and Vince can hear the men
rummaging through items in the kitchen and dining room. It isn't until
they drag the body of Dr. Blythworth inside from the front porch that
they see the two men who are inside their house. They back away from
the stairs.

                    VINCE
So, what do you think?

                    MARIAM
I don't know, sweetie. I really don't. I mean...at first I thought we should
go downstairs and try to get out the front door. But they locked it. Plus,
the time it takes us to creep down the stairs, they might catch us in mid-
step...and we definitely don't want that.

                    VINCE
Yeah.

                    MARIAM
Besides, they killed Dr. Blythworth and I wouldn't put it past them to do
the same to us if they find out we're in the house.

VINCE

What if they already know we're in here?

MARIAM

Well, I really don't think they know we are, 'cause if they did, we would probably be the first thing they looked for, instead of looking for things to steal.

VINCE

What do you think they want, Mariam?

MARIAM

Valuable stuff they can sell, like Mom's jewelry.

VINCE

But, that's up here...where we are.

MARIAM

Yeah, I know...that's the problem. We've gotta find a way to get downstairs and out of the house to call the police. Maybe we should hide in your room since it is the closest room to the staircase, and once they walk down the hall to Mom and Dad's room we can sneak out.

VINCE

You really think that'll work? (Vince clutches his stomach)

MARIAM

I don't know, but...hey, what's wrong?

VINCE

My stomach...it really hurts.

Mariam reaches over and puts her hand on Vince's forehead. She takes Vince by the hand and starts to lead him back to look down the stairs.

MARIAM

Change of plans.

VINCE

What? Why?

MARIAM

You're burning up. We have to get out of here.

Mariam and Vince begin to slowly descend the stairs. Mid-way down the stairs, as Mariam puts her weight on a step, it creaks. She holds her breath for a moment, waiting for the two men to race out and find them in the house. But they don't. She lets the breath out and they continue down. As they near the bottom of the stairs, they can hear the two men in the kitchen clinking beer bottles together and laughing about something. Mariam can't make out their words. A few long seconds later they are at the bathroom door. They push it open and rush in. Mariam slowly closes and locks the door. Vince sits down on the toilet seat and is winded and pale. Mariam goes into the medicine cabinet and takes out some children's aspirin and hands them to Vince. Then Mariam gets a glass from the counter and puts some water in it. She hands it to Vince, but it falls to the floor and shatters.

SCENE 16A
SETTING: HOUSE INTERIOR, HALLWAY BY BATHROOM AND KITCHEN
CHARACTERS: JOHN AND NICK

When John and Nick hear the crash, they look at each other for a second and then run out of the kitchen. They reach the entrance way by the front door and stop to listen for movement. They hear none. They start down the hallway in front of them. A door about ten feet in front of the two men slowly opens, and a young girl (Mariam) peeks her head out. Even through the darkness John can make out the whites of the girl's eyes. Mariam ducks back into the bathroom and slams and locks it. The two men run down the hall and start pounding on the bathroom door.

SCENE 16B
SETTING: HOUSE INTERIOR, BATHROOM
CHARACTERS: MARIAM AND VINCE

VINCE

Oh my god! What are we gonna do now? You locked the door, right?

MARIAM

(Pulling her brother close to her and sitting on the floor at the other end of the room) Yeah.

The men continue to pound on the door.

VINCE

Mariam! What are we gonna do?

Mariam shakes her head.

VINCE

What, Mariam? What?

MARIAM

(Impatient and scared) I don't know!

VINCE

(Tears forming in his eyes and slowly running down both cheeks) You don't know? I'm scared, Mariam!

MARIAM

I am too, Vince. I don't know what to do. We're trapped.

SCENE 16A
SETTING: HOUSE INTERIOR, HALLWAY BY BATHROOM AND KITCHEN
CHARACTERS: JOHN AND NICK

After a few minutes the two men stop pounding.

NICK

Shit, man. I think that little bitch saw my face.

JOHN

Ah, don't worry about it, man.

NICK

What do you mean, "don't worry about it"? She *saw* me!

JOHN

Like I said...don't worry about it. She'll never tell.

NICK

Oh, yeah? What makes you so sure?

JOHN

'Cause...I won't let her have a chance to.

John puts his finger up to his lips and motions for Nick to follow him back into the kitchen.

NICK

What you looking for, man?

JOHN

Something to keep those kids where they are...I saw something that I think will work somewhere in one of these drawers.

Nick follows John over to the kitchen counter and watches as he starts to pull open one drawer after the other. After a few minutes John pulls something that looks like rope out of a drawer and holds it up for Nick to see.

NICK

A rope?

JOHN

Not quite. An extension cord...I figure it will work just as well.

NICK

How the hell are we gonna tie them up if we can't even get in?

                                JOHN
We're not going to tie them up, per se, but this'll keep them right where
we want them…until we're ready for them.

Nick follows John back out of the kitchen until they are standing outside
the bathroom door again.

                                NICK
So, what you gonna do?

                                JOHN
Watch and learn, my friend.

John ties one end of the extension cord to the bathroom doorknob and
he stretches it across the hallway and ties the other end to the laundry
room doorknob. He shakes it a few times and then turns around to face
Nick smiling.

                                NICK
Nice.

                                JOHN
Yeah, this should keep 'em right where we want 'em till we're ready.

They walk out of the hallway and turn to go upstairs.

SCENE 17
SETTING: HOUSE INTERIOR, KIDS' BEDROOMS
CHARACTERS: JOHN AND NICK

John and Nick enter Vince's bedroom.

                                NICK
Well this must be one of the kids' rooms.

                                JOHN
Yeah, the little one.

NICK

Yeah.

JOHN

So, unless you want some stuffed animals or a unicorn figurine, we probably won't find anything of value in here.

They walk out of the room and enter the one across the hallway. This one is darker than the last room they were in, as it doesn't have a night light on. But, from the moon light coming in from the windows, Nick notices that it must be the older of the two kid's room.

NICK

Hey, John.

JOHN

Yeah?

NICK

You think anything good will be in here?

JOHN

Only one way to find out…you check the dresser and nightstand drawers and I'll check out that desk over there.

NICK

Cool.

John watches Nick walk over to the dresser and start looking through its drawers. He goes over to the desk and starts looking through the various papers scattered on top. He pulls out the top side drawer of the desk and takes his pen light from his pocket and shines it inside. The light bounces back at him. Sitting in the back of the drawer is a small box with gold details etched on its top. He opens it to find a few small jewels. He pulls it out, closes the drawer, and sets the box on top of the desk.

NICK

What'd you find? Nothin' in her dresser but clothes.

JOHN

Don't know yet. But, could be good. Looks like the little shit tried to hide it pretty well. Come on over and check it out.

Nick joins John at the desk. John opens the box and shines his light in. He almost shrieks for joy at seeing what was inside the box.

NICK

Damn.

JOHN

Yup. Jackpot!

Inside the box are several rings, bracelets, and necklaces. John motions for Nick to open the bag they had brought upstairs.

JOHN

I don't know about some of this stuff...but most of this is the real McCoy.

NICK

Might as well take it all and sort through it later.

JOHN

Now you're learning, buddy.

John picks up the gold box and dumps the remaining contents into the bag. He then shrugs and throws in the box for good measure.

JOHN

Not sure if that box is real gold or not, but like my momma used to say, "better safe than sorry."

NICK

Your momma sounds like a smart woman.

JOHN

Damn straight.

They search the rest of the room but don't find anything else. They return to the hallway and start walking toward the master bedroom. They hear a crash and freeze in their tracks.

SCENE 18
SETTING: HOUSE INTERIOR, BATHROOM
CHARACTERS: MARIAM AND VINCE

Mariam stands back from the shattered bathroom window and turns to her brother.

MARIAM
Okay, Vince. Here's the plan. I'm going to go out first. Once I get out there and down to the ground, you climb up on the toilet and then shimmy yourself out the window and I'll catch you from below.

VINCE
Don't you think it would be better if I go first?

MARIAM
I thought about that, but no. It's at least a ten-foot drop from the window to the ground, and I don't want you busting an ankle or something when you land.

VINCE
I can make it.

MARIAM
I don't really want to take a chance on you getting hurt.

VINCE
Getting *hurt* is a lot better than what happened to poor Dr. Blythworth.

MARIAM
Yeah, that's true. But still. I really think it's better for me to go first and be out there to catch you, and we don't have time to argue about it.

VINCE
Alright. Whatever you say.

MARIAM

Hand me a towel or something to put across the bottom of the window frame so we don't get all gashed up by all this broken glass.

Vince pulls a large towel from the cabinet. Mariam takes it from him and drapes it over the bottom of the window frame. She climbs up onto the toilet.

MARIAM

Alright, here goes.

Mariam is halfway out the window when the kids hear something on the other side of the bathroom door. As she shimmies her way out the window and is about ready to jump to the ground, the bathroom door explodes open and the two men rush in. She falls out the window.

Mariam hits the ground with her feet, hard, does a somersault, and stands up. She looks up and sees her brother trying to get through the window. His head is hanging out. His arms are flailing up and down. He is screaming.

VINCE

Mariam! No, please! Don't touch me! MOM!

He is pulled back into the room away from the broken window.

MARIAM

You dirty bastards! Let my brother go!

Mariam hears the two men laughing and then one of them pokes his head out of the broken window. It is too dark to make out what he looks like, though Mariam can tell the man has long hair and the slight breeze was blowing it into his face. He calls out to her.

JOHN

Here…little…piggy…piggy…piggy…

MARIAM

Go to hell!

JOHN

Oh, what language from such a cute little girl. You better be a good little girl, or I'll gut your brother like a fish.

MARIAM

You'll do no such thing! He's just a little boy.

JOHN

Oh, you'd be surprised what I'm capable of if I don't get what I want. The stuff in your parents' house is only part of why we picked this house. The other stuff…well…your brother will find out soon enough.

The man laughs and disappears inside the house. Mariam can hear Vince inside the house pleading with the two men to stop touching him, to let him go. Mariam takes off and runs to the back of the house. When she gets to the back of the house, she notices that one of the windows on the back door is broken out. She quietly goes up to the back door, pushes it open and looks inside. She can't see or hear the two men or her brother anywhere. She then carefully reaches in and picks up the phone off its base and quickly punches in 9-1-1 before stretching the cord so that she can lean up against the house, out of sight of the two men if they should wander back into the kitchen. She puts the phone up to her ear, waiting for the 911 operator to pick up, but the voice doesn't come. She doesn't hear anything at all coming from the phone. She peeks around the corner of the door and, not seeing anyone, quickly hangs the phone up, picks it up again and taps in the same three numbers. She puts the phone up to her ear again. Nothing. The line is dead. She leans back up against the side of the house and puts her hands over her face trying to keep it together.

SCENE 19
SETTING: HOUSE INTERIOR, HALLWAY AND VINCE'S BEDROOM

CHARACTERS: JOHN, NICK, VINCE

With a hand over Vince's mouth, John pulls him, kicking and screaming, from the bathroom and into the hallway. He nods to Nick to pick up the boy's feet and help him carry him upstairs. They carry him in and lay him on the bed.

JOHN

Find something to tie him up with.

NICK

Okay.

After searching, Nick holds up a pair of old shoes. The laces are untied and dangling.

NICK

How's this?

JOHN

That'll work. Find another pair. We'll use them for each of his arms and legs and tie them to the bedposts. He won't be going anywhere then.

NICK

Nice.

After finding another pair of shoes, Nick removes all the laces and hands two of them to John. John begins to tie the boy's wrists to the bedposts, while Nick works on his ankles. John picks up a sock that is lying on the floor and stuffs it in the boy's mouth.

JOHN

That'll keep him from yappin'.

When all the boy's limbs are tied off and the sock in his mouth is secure, John nods to Nick, turns off the night light and walks out of the room, shutting the door behind them.

JOHN

That should keep him from getting away.

NICK

Yeah...but, what in the hell are we gonna do with him?

JOHN

Hummm...well...that's a good question. Actually, we can do whatever we want with him. We can kill him outright *or* we can have some fun with him first, maybe cut him a little...see how much he screams...there's a ton of possibilities with something like this.

NICK

You're one sick puppy, you know that, don't you?

JOHN

Yup. Proud of it, too.

They start down the hall toward the stairs.

NICK

One question, though. Why do we have to kill him at all? I mean, shit, he looks scared half to death, ya know? It's not like he'll be a reliable witness, the traumatized little boy that he'll be.

JOHN

Hey, you're the one that was just bitchin' a while ago about them seeing your face and shit. Now you wanna just let him live? Fuck that. That little shit is gonna die a slow death if I have anything to say about it. But first...we gotta find his older sister.

NICK

Yeah...okay...I guess you're right.

JOHN

Damn straight I'm right. Listen, I've done this dozens of times. The most important thing my mentor taught me, and what you better get in your head, is that you never leave someone alive that might be able to identify you. Hell, you don't start doing shit like that, no matter if you think they're too scared to tell on you or not, you just don't take that chance.

NICK

Yeah. Okay. So what's next? How do we find his older sister?

Nick walks behind John down the stairs.

JOHN

Well, the way I see it…she'll be somewhere around the house still. Maybe not inside the house, but she'll be around somewhere, maybe hiding out in the garage or behind some bushes in the back yard or something. I know one thing for sure…

NICK

What's that?

JOHN

A sibling is never going to leave the other one to die. And I imagine from the older one seeing how we did the dude on the porch earlier she's not going to take the chance to venture far from the house to call the cops. 'Cause if you think about it, in her mind we're probably killing her brother right now, or at least talking about how to do it. And if I were her, I wouldn't want to take that chance, ya know?

NICK

Yeah…guess that does make some sense.

JOHN

Now come on.

SCENE 20
SETTING: HOUSE EXTERIOR BY BACK DOOR, INTERIOR KITCHEN
CHARACTERS: JOHN, NICK, MARIAM

Mariam is still hiding just outside the back door when she hears the two men enter the kitchen. She squats down to the ground and holds her breath, trying to make out what is being said.

JOHN

Alright, this is what we'll do.

John grabs Nick's beer off the counter and hands it to him. Nick takes a sip.

JOHN

We'll split up and search for the little bitch.

NICK

Sounds simple enough.

JOHN

Yeah, it does. But remember, if you don't know your opponent, things can turn sour in a hurry.

NICK

Come on, John. What is the girl, fifteen, sixteen at the most? How hard can it be?

JOHN

You'd be surprised. Just keep your wits about you when we split up. If you have the chance to bag her, do it. But, if she has some sort of weapon, call me and I'll come runnin'.

NICK

Come runnin' with what?

JOHN

This. (He pulls a closed straight razor out of his pocket and flips it open to reveal a long, shiny blade)

NICK

Nice.

JOHN

You damn right, buddy. This was Rock's blade.

NICK

I thought you told me once that he was taken down by the cops.

JOHN

Oh, yeah, he was alright. But...I have a buddy that works for the cops, and he was able to get it outta the evidence room for me.

NICK

Nice. It's cool and all that you have a blade and such, but don't you think it would be a good idea if I carry something, too?

JOHN

Yeah, probably not a bad idea at all. (pointing to a large butcher rack filled with knives) Pick your poison.

NICK

Ohhh…preeety.

Nick laughs and then selects the longest one in the rack, the butcher knife. He draws it out, moves it up to his face, and twists it from side to side. The moon light coming in through the window glints off the blade.

NICK

Yeah, I think this will work just fine.

JOHN

Good. Now, let's get to it. You take the house and I'll search the yard and garage.

SCENE 21A
SETTING: HOUSE EXTERIOR BY BACK DOOR AND GARAGE
CHARACTERS: JOHN, MARIAM

Mariam pushes herself off the house and makes her way to the front of the house. She finds the side door to the garage unlocked and pushes the door open, entering the dark confines of the garage. She finds a flashlight and searches through her father's tools for a weapon. She finds a long metal file and turns back toward the door. Before she can reach it, the door flies open. Startled, Mariam drops the flashlight, but for a split second she sees the long-haired man (John) carrying a straight razor step inside the garage. The room goes black. Mariam screams.

SCENE 22A
SETTING: HOUSE INTERIOR
CHARACTERS: VINCE

Even though he is inside the house and tied down to his bed, Vince hears the scream. He can tell it came from outside the house. He knew it was his sister. Knowing that at least one of the two men had caught Mariam makes a lump form in his throat. He begins to cry. He starts to jerk his arms and legs this way and that, trying to free himself. After a while, the knot in the shoelace that holds his right wrist to the bedpost begins to loosen.

SCENE 23A
SETTING: HOUSE INTERIOR, LIVING ROOM, EXTERIOR BACK YARD
CHARACTERS: NICK

Nick is searching for the girl in the living room when he hears the scream from the garage. He takes off running. As he nears the front door, he hesitates, thinking about using it to go outside, but thinks better of it. He takes off running toward the back door instead. He staggers out the back door and starts running; though he isn't exactly sure where the scream had come from, he figures it came from the garage. Arms and legs pumping, he holds the large butcher knife tightly in his right hand, ready for whatever lay ahead.

SCENE 21B
SETTING: GARAGE
CHARACTERS: JOHN AND MARIAM

The garage is pitch black. Mariam can hear the muffled breathing of the long-haired man somewhere in the garage, but can't see him. She continues to inch her way around. As she moves through the garage,

Mariam tries to keep some of her senses on the man's breathing and his approximate location. Something brushes against her forehead and she screams. Her rump hits the floor. She silently gets to a crouched position and moves locations. The man's breathing continues to fill the dark garage.

SCENE 23B
SETTING: EXTERIOR BACK YARD
CHARACTERS: NICK, A STRANGER (MR. HENDERSON)

As Nick runs through the back yard, he hears the second scream and picks up his pace. He can see the side door of the garage. As he bolts toward it, the back side of a shovel crashes against his face and he crumbles to the ground.

SCENE 21C
SETTING: GARAGE
CHARACTERS: JOHN AND MARIAM

Mariam can tell from his breathing, getting closer and closer, that the man was coming. She continues to inch her way through the darkness again. She hears the man laugh then speak.

JOHN
Here, little piggy, piggy, piggy…come out, come out, come out…wherever you are.

MARIAM
Shut up!

JOHN
Ah, come on now. I promise I won't hurt you.

MARIAM
Yeah, right. Why are you doing this?

Between phrases, Mariam finds items in the garage and throws them away from herself to confuse the man about her location. She continues to search the darkness in front of her with her arms. Her left shin bangs against something. She wants to scream out and grab her throbbing leg, but she knows if she does that it means she would have to stop walking.

JOHN
Ah, come on now. You're not mad at me...are you?

Mariam hears the question loud and clear. She also hears the man stifle a chuckle after saying it. Even though she knows she shouldn't, she can't help but respond.

MARIAM
You *are* a real prick, ya know that?

JOHN
Just call me John.

MARIAM
Okay. John.

JOHN
And your name is, my dear?

MARIAM
Mariam.

JOHN
Ohhh...what a pretty name for a pretty little piggy.

John laughs and Miriam takes a firm grip on the metal file.

SCENE 24A
SETTING: CAR INTERIOR, NIGHT
CHARACTERS: ROBERT AND JULIA (THE KIDS' PARENTS)

Robert looks over at his wife and can tell she is nervous and scared. He reaches over and strokes the back of her neck. She turns her head toward him. Her words come out in a whisper.

JULIA

Robby, do you really think the kids are in trouble?

ROBERT

I don't know, Julia. I really don't. But that message the front desk gave us from a neighbor was definitely strange enough to worry me that they might not be okay. And not getting a call through worries me.

JULIA

Oh my god...what are we gonna do if something has happened to them?

ROBERT

I don't know, sweetheart. I really don't.

JULIA

What if they're really in trouble or hurt or one of them is...

ROBERT

Now, now...

Robert reaches behind Julia and begins stroking her neck again.

SCENE 22B
SETTING: HOUSE INTERIOR
CHARACTERS: VINCE

Vince starts to work on the knot holding his right ankle against the bed frame. Frustrated, he collapses back onto the bed.

SCENE 21D
SETTING: GARAGE
CHARACTERS: JOHN AND MARIAM

The man's breathing sounds closer. Mariam starts to move again.

Cobwebs brush through her hair, something bounces off her forehead. She almost screams again until she realizes it is just the golf ball fashioned by her father to the rope which leads up to the attic above the garage. She reaches up to grab the rope, but at the same time a pair of hands grab her and she is pulled away from her temporary escape from the long-haired man.

SCENE 24B
SETTING: CAR INTERIOR, NIGHT
CHARACTERS: ROBERT AND JULIA

Robert looks down at the dash of the Mercedes then over at his wife.

ROBERT

Honey, how are you doing?

JULIA

How the hell do you think I am doing, Robert? Our kids are in trouble, and we still have a long way to go until we're home.

ROBERT

They'll be okay, Julia.

JULIA

How can you be so sure?

ROBERT

Because I have faith that Mariam can take care of the house and of Vince or I wouldn't have agreed to this weekend. Besides, for all we know, our *neighbor* that supposedly saw whatever they think they saw could have the whole thing blown out of proportion.

JULIA

I hope you're right.

ROBERT

(Pondering) I could try Bill Henderson again and have him go over and check on the kids. Although I know how the kids, or at least Mariam, feels about him. She would never forgive us if nothing is wrong and I have Bill go over and knock on the door and ask if everything is okay.

JULIA

They will just have to get over it. I still think we should call the police.

ROBERT

Julia, we don't know that there is even anything to worry about. All we know is a neighbor called and said there was suspicious activity at the house. If we call the police and it turns out to just be the kids' friends, what will that make us look like? Not only stupid, but also like we don't trust Mariam. Let me just call Bill.

Robert makes the call. Julia watches him intently. He hangs up, and Julia sinks. No answer. Robert presses down on the accelerator and the needle on the speedometer climbs to eighty. He sees red and blue in his rearview.

ROBERT

Shit me sideways!

JULIA

What?

ROBERT

Cop.

Robert eases his right foot off the gas pedal and watches the needle on the speedometer start to go down. Julia starts to cry.

SCENE 21E
SETTING: GARAGE
CHARACTERS: JOHN AND MARIAM

Mariam comes to and is tied down to her father's work bench. Her arms and legs are tied to the table's legs. She tries to move them, but can't. She is able to move her head. There is some night light filtering in through the garage windows, but she can't see anyone else in the room with her. A voice breaks the silence.

JOHN

Looks like I got me a prime cut of hog right here. Oh, yes. A *very* prime cut, if I do day so myself. Yummy in my tummy.

MARIAM

(Quietly) Sick bastard.

JOHN

Huh. What was that, my little piggy?

MARIAM

I said, you are one sick BASTARD!

JOHN

Hey, hey now. What did I tell you about your mouth? I mean, I like my ladies dirty and all, but not with such sewage spewing out of their hole.

MARIAM

Fuck you!

JOHN

Tisk, tisk, tisk...

MARIAM

Shut up!

JOHN

Oh, come on now, it won't be that bad.

MARIAM

What won't be *that* bad?

ROBERT

When I cut you up and eat you like the little piggy that you are, of course.

A *clack* is heard and a bright light fills the room.

SCENE 25
SETTING: HOUSE INTERIOR
CHARACTERS: MR. HENDERSON AND VINCE

Mr. Henderson sees the broken glass from the back door and silently enters the house. He notices the open beer bottles and moves out of the kitchen and through the dining room. In the entry, he sees a dead man (Dr. Blythworth) lying on the floor, his neck has been slashed. The blood is now coagulating, and there are red streak marks indicating the body had been moved at some point. Moving past the body, he enters the living room and begins to look around. The television and lights are off. It doesn't look like there had been any sort of struggle inside the room. He exits the living room, turns and walks down a narrow hallway. Nearing the end of the hallway, he notices the extension cord. He enters the bathroom. The window is open (broken). A cool breeze is drifting into the room, fluttering the open curtain. Exiting the bathroom and turning right, he walks back down the hallway and starts up the dark staircase. He gets to the top of the stairs and notices a partially open door on the right. Slowly moving to the door, he leans an ear close to the door. There isn't anyone talking or doing *anything* in the room, but he lowers the shovel to a "ready" position, and shoves the door the rest of the way open. Vince screams. He smiles.

SCENE 21E
SETTING: GARAGE
CHARACTERS: JOHN AND MARIAM

Mariam sees the long-haired man, a twisted grin stretched across his narrow face. He licks his lips as he stares into Mariam's eyes. He is clearly aroused.

JOHN
You're a very beautiful young lady, you know that, don't you?

Mariam just stares at him.

JOHN
Sure, you do. Hell, I just saw you the other day when me and my buddy were casing out the joint. You were out in the driveway washing a slick looking Mercedes. You really soaped that sucker up. Man, just the way

you were bent over the hood and moved that sponge around in circles made me wanna...and your hips, oh god, your hips...they moved in synch with that music you were listening to. You're a real piece of prime cut meat...but, you know that. Hell, sure you do. You wouldn't be parading that body of yours in that bikini in front of the house for any passersby to see if you didn't already know that.

MARIAM

I wasn't doing anything but washing the car.

JOHN

Anyway (moving slowly toward her), you really are hot. I wonder if you feel as good as you look.

SCENE 26A
SETTING: HOUSE INTERIOR
CHARACTERS: MR. HENDERSON AND VINCE

Vince and Mr. Henderson quietly walk down the stairs.

SCENE 21F
SETTING: GARAGE
CHARACTERS: JOHN AND MARIAM

MARIAM

Don't you dare touch me, you filthy piece of trash.

The long-haired man begins to run his rough hands up her calves.

JOHN

Hummm...mighty smooth legs you got here. (licking his lips)

He moves his hands up to Mariam's thighs and moans.

JOHN

God, you are so beautiful. Shame I'm gonna have to kill such a sweet young thing as yourself.

MARIAM

But…but, why? You don't have to kill me, mister. Hey, listen. I swear if you just take what you want out of the house and leave me and my brother alone, I won't tell anybody about what happened here. Okay?

The man laughs.

JOHN

You really think I'm gonna believe that, huh? Here is what's going to happen, okay. I'm gonna have a little fun with you, and then your brother, and then me and my friend Nick are going to steal all your parents' shit. Now, how does *that* sound?

MARIAM

Sounds like *shit*.

JOHN

(Laughing) Well, I don't think you're in any position to make any requests or demands now, are ya?

SCENE 26B
SETTING: HOUSE INTERIOR AND BACK YARD
CHARACTERS: MR. HENDERSON, VINCE, NICK

Vince and Mr. Henderson walk through the silent house. They hear Mariam scream. They stop and listen for another scream, but one doesn't come. He waves for Vince to follow him into the back yard. Another scream rips through the air. Vince clutches onto Mr. Henderson's arm. He follows him along the side of the house. When he comes to the corner of the house, next to the garage, he abruptly stops. Vince nearly runs into his back.

VINCE

(Whispering) What?

He wants to turn around and tell him the guy he had hit with the shovel earlier was still unconscious and on the ground. But he can't. The man is gone and so is the large butcher knife he had been carrying. Mr. Henderson takes a deep breath and turns around just in time to see a dark shadow coming up behind Vince. His knife is the only thing about the man that Mr. Henderson can make out. Mr. Henderson wants to scream out to warn Vince of the oncoming man, but can't.

VINCE

Well?

Then the man's knife plunges deep into his back and he lets out a blood curdling scream.

SCENE 24C
SETTING: CAR INTERIOR, NIGHT
CHARACTERS: ROBERT AND JULIA

Robert looks over at his wife and watches her continue to bite her nails. He takes her hand and tries to offer a reassuring smile.

ROBERT

Almost home, Hon.

SCENE 21G
SETTING: GARAGE
CHARACTERS: JOHN AND MARIAM

Mariam lay on the table, her shirt torn open. The long-haired man is on top of her and looks toward the garage door.

JOHN

(Muttering) Yum, sounds like more meat.

He looks irritated as he climbs off Mariam. She looks relieved. He pulls the closed straight razor from his pocket and walks out the door.

SCENE 26C
SETTING: HOUSE EXTERIOR, BACK YARD
CHARACTERS: MR. HENDERSON, VINCE, NICK

Vince lies on his stomach in the grass. Nick is sprawled on his back, making it impossible for him to push himself off the ground. The knife is still lodged in his back. The man wiggles the blade around in circles. Vince screams. He tries to lift his face off the ground to look for Mr. Henderson, but Nick pushes his head down with his other hand. Suddenly the man flies backwards through the air. He is still holding the knife in his hand, and Vince screams again as it is ripped from his back. He lands a few feet away. Mr. Henderson runs over, lifts the spade high into the air and brings it straight down. As the blade pierces the man's neck, there is a crack and a wet *thunk*. Then Mr. Henderson brings back one of his boots and kicks the man's face. There is a *thud*, like a cantaloupe being stomped on, and then the head flies through the air into the dark back yard. Mr. Henderson runs back over to Vince. He has rolled over onto his back. Mr. Henderson holds a hand out to him.

MR. HENDERSON
Can you stand? We need to get you some help.

VINCE
Please, help Mariam first.

Out of nowhere, John charges Mr. Henderson and tackles him to the ground. A long straight razor is imbedded in the front of Mr. Henderson's neck. Vince runs.

SCENE 21H
SETTING: GARAGE AND BACK YARD

CHARACTERS: MARIAM, VINCE, MR. HENDERSON, NICK AND JOHN

Mariam struggles against her ties. When she gets nowhere, she closes her eyes and screams out in frustration. When she opens her eyes, Vince is staring down at her. He is sheathed in blood.

VINCE

Mariam, are you okay?

MARIAM

I'm fine. Can you untie me? Oh, God, Vince, you're bleeding.

VINCE

(Untying his sister) Shhh...hush. The one with the long hair is still out there. We have to get out of here.

Mariam gets off the table and helps her weakening brother out the side door of the garage. When they enter the back yard, Mariam's mouth falls open. She can't believe the carnage that lay in front of her. In the middle of the yard, she sees the bodies of both of the men and of a man she recognizes as Mr. Henderson from across the street.

MARIAM

Oh my God.

VINCE

Mr. Henderson rescued me and killed that guy, but the other one killed him.

The long-haired man is lying on top of the burglar who had lost his head. There are several long deep gashes across the man's back. Mariam starts to cry and seems in shock until she feels Vince start to slide down. Mariam pulls him up and holds him tightly.

MARIAM

Hold on, Vince. We are going to get help now. Everything's going to be alright. Come on.

Brightness suddenly fills the strip of yard in between the house and the garage. Mariam smiles slightly and leads Vince in the direction of their parents' car and they walk *together* toward the light.

www.ingramcontent.com/pod-product-compliance
Lightning Source LLC
Chambersburg PA
CBHW020625250626
47154CB00004B/1667